UNCHIPPED:
THE RESORT

UNCHIPPED:
THE RESORT

TAYA DEVERE

DVM Press
Vaakunatie 16 D 14
20780 Kaarina, Suomi-Finland
www.dvmpress.com
www.tayadevere.com

For information about special discounts available for bulk purchases, sales promotions, fund-raising and educational needs, contact sales@dvmpress.com

ISBN 978-952-7404-14-0 First Ebook Edition
ISBN 978-952-7404-15-7 First Print Edition

Cover Design © 2020 by Deranged Doctor Design -
www.derangeddoctordesign.com
Ebook formatting by Polgarus Studios – www.polgarusstudios.com
Editing by Christopher Scott Thompson and Lindsay Fara Kaplan

To all underdogs out there:
The black sheep, the odd ducks, the rejects, the loners.
You make this world go around.

THE BEST OF ME

A short story in the world of the Unchipped series

The club is buzzing with dancing people and music. Glitter, feathers, and wild hair glimmer in the neon lights. When the song changes to another beat—almost identical to the previous one—the lights go off for a moment. The moment is long enough that Dennis has to stop walking because he can't see. Can't risk bumping into a bar stool. To stumble and hit his head is hardly something a desirable bachelor like himself should do. But even if he did—his damn near perfect face and body wouldn't break or scar. He couldn't hurt himself, not even if he tried.

Not in this reality.

The lights blaze on again. Dennis adjusts his Stetson and continues his walk. His cowboy boots clunk against the sticky bar floor—he can hear the sound over the loud music. They've improved the sound effects since the last time he visited—which was only last night.

At the back of the bar, a woman with bright orange

lipstick crosses her bare legs. Her long blond hair reaches her navel, thick locks wrapping around her curves like a possessive albino snake. Thirty-one, maybe thirty-two. That's how old she's decided to be tonight. Dennis raises the two bottles of beer in his hand, moves the toothpick from one side of his mouth to the other. Even in a fake reality it seems odd to sit down with a stranger without a drink in his hand.

"Hell of a line, doll. Hope you're not parched."

A perfect row of pearl-white teeth competes with the bar's light show. Her face is impossibly symmetrical, her skin flawless. Eyes coral blue, she winks at Dennis and accepts one of the beer bottles, but doesn't take a sip. Why would she?

"Well, aren't you just the perfect gentleman." She undresses Dennis with her eyes as he sits, well aware of her admiring gaze on his tan and toned body. He knows what works in this room: well-fitted jeans and a few open buttons.

"So, tell me, stallion. How old are you?"

Dennis cocks his head and narrows his eyes while his smile deepens. Today, his eyes are the deepest brown the AR-store has to offer. "Thirty-five, doll. It was my birthday last week."

Her full orange lips give him another smile. She pretends to take a sip of the beer Dennis has bought her. "And how many times has it been, cutie-pie?"

"How many times, what?"

"That you've turned thirty-five?"

Dennis's eyes drill into hers, estimating. Her choice of orange lipstick tells him she's young enough to feel the need to stand out. Bold. Revealing dress, flawless face… she's a rookie for sure. An older woman would know better: Men need flaws. A scar, maybe an extra pound on the waist, maybe two. Slightly crooked teeth, that sort of thing. Perfection doesn't arouse him. No— it's boring. But tonight, he's been drawn in by that long, blond hair. Might as well sit down and keep this one on the hook while he scans for someone better.

There would be more to choose from, if it wasn't for the newest nighty-night-pill, released and delivered by the City of California to its citizens earlier today. Actually, it's surprising that the room is even this full. People call it a night hours before they usually would, hoping for a new and stronger kind of high. It's surprising that there are this many people out and about, AR-socializing instead of snoozing away in a newly-found state of Zen. During a new pill launch, it's not uncommon for the rooms to echo with emptiness.

"Well?" She pouts, makes a face which she's practiced in front of the selfie-lens for hours on end. Dennis can tell. He's no rookie.

"Why is it," Dennis asks, "that age is the first thing we ask each other? Not whether we're happy in life. Or what we do when we're not working. When's the last time we cried? Who is your role model?"

"Wow," the woman says. "That old, huh?"

She's young—much younger than what he'd

prefer—but he doesn't want to be alone. Not tonight. He gives her his best smile and leans forward on his seat. He knows she can see his well-built chest this way. "Let's just say this is not my first rodeo."

A flicker in her eye.

Hand playing with a loose lock of too-white hair.

A giggle.

He almost wishes he would fail. Just this once. Challenge, that's what he needs. Not easy pickings.

A low buzzing sound interrupts Dennis and breaks their gaze. Three white dots appear at the corner of his vision. An AR-call. This late at night, it can only be one person. No one else would dare interrupt his night.

"Will you excuse me, doll? I need to step outside for a moment."

She cocks her head, lifts her chin to reveal her long, fragile-looking neck. "It's not a booty-call, is it, Daddy?"

Maybe she really is *too* young. The ones with daddy issues always are.

"Business call," he says and raises his hand. Before he taps the side of the AR-glasses to leave the simulation, he adds, "Sit tight, doll."

He hopes she won't listen. That she'll at least pretend to play hard to get.

"A mole? You're sure?"

Dennis paces by the balcony railing. He gulps some

cold water to sober himself up. The green city opens in front of him, dark and eerie, the neon lights flashing and flickering wildly. The commercials never end—not even when there's no one to watch them. It's three a.m.. Thanks to the newest government-issued drug, the city is unconscious, enjoying peaceful and restorative sleep.

"Ah, Dennis," she says. He can nearly hear the woman smile at the other end of the line. She hasn't turned the video on and isn't a fan of the hologram-calls. "Your Texas accent. It's fading, my dear."

"Not many people to talk to these days. It happens. Things fade."

"Not even those young girls in the SIM dating rooms? How is *The Best of Me* treating you, anyway?"

How does she know about that? Dennis should be too high in the program's hierarchy, too important for surveillance.

"No, we're not tracking you."

"Then, how…"

"Little birds. I asked what you wanted for your birthday. Nurse Saarinen gave me the tip. Said you had cursed the selection in the dating rooms during new happiness-pill launches."

"That I did," Dennis admits. "It's mostly men out there, I'm afraid."

"Or women choosing to be men…"

"Even worse. Not sure why anyone would do that?"

She laughs, her voice soft and tempting. If only Laura Solomon wasn't his boss—everyone's boss—he would have made a move a long time ago. Maybe right after Claudia had—

"So, anyway. I told Nurse Saarinen to shut down all the other rooms for tonight. Happy birthday, Texas."

That's why there had been so many people tonight, despite the happiness-pill launch. They had nowhere else to go.

"You calling me that sounds odd," he says. "Only the people in the mansion usually call me that."

"Yeah, well. Suits you. *Texas*." She hums happily. Dennis swallows and waits for her to go on. "Wanted to try it out, is all."

They both fall silent for a few seconds. Dennis wets his lips, wanting to ask something from her in return. Something personal. Her likes and dislikes. What kind of flowers—

"How is the new mansion crew coming along?"

She beats him to it. The moment is gone.

Dennis leans against the metal railing, gazing down onto the streets. No self-driving limos with dimmed windows. No Unchipped pedestrians, making their way to Texas's building for a quick meeting. That's all the movement you see on a normal day. Then again, who is he to decide what's normal anyway?

"Dennis? Bad connection?"

"No, no. I'm here."

"And the mansion?"

He exhales, turns around and walks back to his gaming chair. Minding his tweaked back, he sits gingerly on the leather seat. The chair creaks under his weight. The black coverall he's wearing feels tight around his belly area. "The progress would be smoother if I got my girl back."

Doctor Solomon stays quiet.

"I know, I know. We're not there yet. And once we are, she'll need an immense amount of training and alteration, and I agree. It's just... Maria was the one to keep the ball rolling. The others were more or less useless compared to her."

"Even William?"

It's Dennis' turn to brood. He had enjoyed Bill's company. Had big hopes for him. His design work had been second to none, and the man had never lost his ambitious ways—no matter how rich and powerful he was getting. For someone like Bill to jump ship had been a shock. Never during Dennis' thirty years of managing a mega-corporation has he seen a change of heart quite so sudden and so completely out of character. Or had he just missed the signs? Had living in the AR life, his environment responding to his every desire, conditioned him to see what he wished to see?

"I wouldn't mind finding William. Maybe bringing him back to work for me, after a short visit to Nurse Saarinen's mind augmentation project."

"Might take quite a lot more than a short visit. Your CEO basically leads the rebels now."

"And where are we with that? Stopping the rebels? I know you vetoed our most effective option, but don't you think it's about time we made a move? That was a hell of a lot of CC's those bastards stole from us."

"First things first, dear. As you now know," Doctor Solomon says. "We have a mole, and it turns out this traitor has been helping our rebel crew since the shit hit the fan at Kinship Care."

"The mole is in City of England?"

"We think so. Iris called, from City of Serbia. She's the one who found the malware in the system and spotted the devices that had been tampered with."

"Good girl."

"Mm. Gave her a raise and put her in charge of the purple city."

"Well-deserved." Dennis shakes his tipsy head, not believing he has yet to ask the most burning question. "Hold on. Who's the mole?"

"Margaret."

"Margaret from the accounting department?"

"No. Margaret from IT."

"Lewis?"

"Yes."

"Fuck me."

"Agreed."

Solomon gives him a moment to let the thought sink in. One of their own—a founder—working with the rebels? Margaret had always been difficult, but in the past the issue was the children. She and Mrs. Salonen had pushed for youth rights ever since the Happiness-Program first got legs. The deaf woman had finally gotten her way, on the condition that she would finalize her research on singularity and mind augmentation. Everyone was surprised when she had agreed. Even more surprising was that the old woman—Laura's mother, Mrs. Salonen—didn't put up a fight. In fact, that had been the moment when Mrs. Salonen had stopped coming to the meetings and demanding updates on the healing capsules she'd invented. No one ever asked Laura what had happened to her mother, and she never mentioned her. In the end, everyone was more relieved than curious, for Mrs. Salonen had been a force to be reckoned with.

"We must find her, Dennis. You know this, right?"

Her words snap him back to this moment. "Who? Margaret?"

"Sure. But I'm talking about the Unchipped girl. Kaarina and her little crew. Your William. The kids."

"And how—"

"Hold on a second, Dennis. It's Nurse Saarinen. I must take this."

He didn't mean to jump back into *The Best of Me* simulation while waiting for Doctor Solomon's and Nurse Saarinen's AR-call to end. A mole this high in the hierarchy is a bad thing. The news is too important for him to focus on anything else.

Yet here he sits. Staring at a pair of orange lips, fake-sipping beer from an old-fashioned brown bottle. Was that how he had blown his cover? Must be. No thirty-five-year-old would buy a drink like that for his date. He'd go for something modern, just for optics; a neon-colored rainbow cocktail, maybe a mini-fountain-tini. Whiskey-soda with a crushed Happiness-Pill. That sort of thing. But never a brown glass bottle with a one-word-label.

"Sorry, doll. Where were we?"

"Daddy issues."

Dennis crosses his leg on his knee and frowns. He hadn't said that out loud. Had he?

"My daddy issues. You were just about to ask me about them." She fixes her long hair around her body. "Weren't you?"

Dennis looks at the bottle in his hands. He should have gotten a whiskey. Not at the SIM-bar, but in his kitchen while talking with Doctor Solomon.

"I'll tell you my age," the girl says, running her fingers on her neck. "If you ask nicely."

But Dennis doesn't care. He already knows how this night is going to end—if he so desires.

There's nothing wrong with AR-sex. As a matter of a fact, the tickling, head-rushing sensations it brings should in many ways be better than the real deal. Skin on skin. Every soft—or demanding—touch. Every adrenaline driven sigh. Each sound pushing and activating one's lust-driven mind. Each stroke washes through one's being, rushing through every pathway of the somatosensory system, caressing and pressing each neuron and cell as it sinks into one's consciousness. It's flawless. Disease and mess free. Anonymous. Always perfect bodies, always performing, acting, finishing in sync without a fail. But unlike most people—those hooked and plugged into their gaming chairs and AR-lovers' make-believe bodies for twenty-four-seven—to Dennis, this kind of flawless lovemaking leaves him hollow. Empty. Wanting. In fact, he enjoys this part more. What comes *before* the SIM-produced multi-orgasms. And yet, Dennis can't seem to quit the chase.

Without Margaret Lewis turning rogue, they'd already be in the men's toilet, her apple-shaped fake buttocks pressed against the see-through walls. That's what the booths are there for. Because who pisses or shits in an alternate reality? And, of course, no one knows who they are here, so privacy is not at the top of their list of worries.

Cracking his knuckles, Dennis sets the beer bottle between them on the table. Then he nods and gestures for her to do the same. Disheartened to see how eagerly the woman obeys anything he says, Dennis watches her lean over, her round bosom now hovering closer to his face.

Fake and boring, yes. But it works. Dennis finds himself holding his breath until the woman leans back in her chair.

He takes out a hundred-dollar bill. It always makes an impression on them, him carrying old currency with him. Waving it in front of her eyes, he then sets it between the bottles, flat against the table. He turns around and snaps his fingers at a waiter. Unnaturally soon, the waiter brings him a third brown bottle, sets it on the table, and walks away. "Tell you what, doll. If you can figure this out, I'll tell you how old I am. And you can keep the money too."

"But it's—"

"I'll transfer the funds to your CC-account the minute you figure this out."

She crosses her arms against her flat stomach. A defiant smile spreads across her face.

"See this note?" Dennis takes the hundred-dollar bill and sets it on top of the two brown bottles, placed four inches apart. "If you can balance the third bottle on top of the bill, without it or the bottle falling, you win."

The girl stares at the note on top of the two bottles. She leans closer to it, blows on it. The paper money drops onto the table. "That's impossible. Gravity is still a thing, old man. Even in this reality."

The AR-glasses buzz again. Solomon's back, possibly with news.

"Oh, it's possible." Dennis sits back and presses his finger on his glasses. "Five minutes, doll. You can do it."

This time, she turns on the video. Hands folded behind her back, the wind blowing her white lab coat, Laura Solomon stands in the middle of an empty courtyard with yellow grass and dandelions. A field with yellow flowers rises behind her. The camera doesn't show any more of the view than that, but Dennis knows the scenery by heart. He's worked with Doctor Solomon long enough to know she prefers to stay at the headquarters; the Chip-Center in City of Finland.

"What else did Nurse Saarinen say?" he asks, mostly to give himself something else to think about other than the faint wrinkles around Laura's mesmerizing green eyes. The dark smudges under her eyes tells a tale of sleepless nights. It must be challenging to rest when the whole world's well-being is in your hands.

"Oh, not much else. Iris is in charge of the tracking."

"Iris and what army?"

"Exactly that. Don't underestimate the purple city, my dear." Laura looks straight at Dennis. "They've tracked them down before."

"I know the girl is good. And that they've done this before. But can she do it without the Unchipped hacker's help? It's not just Margaret we've lost, Laura."

The woman winces when Dennis calls her by her first name—and her first name only. Only Solomon's right-hand Nurse Saarinen is known to do so. Nurse Saarinen—and Solomon's vanished mother.

Dennis is lucky. She decides to let it slide. "Luna Novak."

"Yes, her. Before the hacker-girl, Iris was always one step behind the rebels."

"I remember." Doctor Solomon opens her mouth to add something but then decides against it.

Dennis gets up from his gaming chair and circles the fake fire that is always blazing—day or night.

"Laura, I hate to sound like a broken record. But isn't it time we move forward? It would be so easy. There are plenty of Chipped who travel with our little crew."

"I know this, dear."

"So, you agree? It is an option?"

"Agreed. It is *an* option."

"And a good one too," Dennis says. "In fact, I don't see why we wouldn't just pull the trigger. These underdogs have caused enough trouble for all of us, don't you think?"

"Hm."

Dennis wants to push the matter further, but he knows it's not wise. Laura Solomon is the kind of person whose silence has more power than her words. When she talks, her words always have a purpose. When she falls silent, her silence is for a reason.

Finally, Solomon turns and starts toward the Chip-Center's back door. "Let me think this through. There's someone there. With them."

"The hacker? Who?"

"No, someone—important. Too important for me to lose."

Who is she talking about? Laura wouldn't care about Kaarina, or Luna the hacker, or any of the chipless kids that ran away from Kinship Care. And in her eyes, the Chipped lost all their value when they fled Laura's city to join the Unchipped rebels. Who would she care

14

about? Enough to hesitate to destroy her enemy?

"Happy birthday, Dennis." She opens the door and walks into a softly glowing blue corridor. Before she clicks off the connection, Laura says, "Now go have some cake."

One of the brown bottles lies on the bar table on its side. The hundred-dollar bill is scrunched into a paper ball. The woman sits pouting, her arms crossed on her full bosom.

Dennis smiles at the girl, who now shows her true age. Nothing has changed in her looks, but her face shows the expression of a young girl, having trouble coping with failure. She hasn't found a way to balance the bottle on top of the note, but she has tried. The spilled beer and slightly damaged money tells the tale.

"No luck then, doll?"

Her eyes drill into him, narrowing with frustration. "I already know you are ancient. I'm already loaded, just like everyone else in this crappy city. Whatever."

Nineteen? Eighteen? he thinks but doesn't ask. They wouldn't let underage users enter the SIM-dating platform. Would they? Dennis feels bad for the girl. Why is she wasting her youth on this? It's different for him—a lonely fifty-five-year-old man. He already has all he needs. Power, money, knowledge. This girl should be out there working on her future, not trying to lure old men into supporting her.

Dennis smiles at her. "Aww, chin up, doll. Nobody gets it the first time."

He takes the paper ball that is his hundred-dollar bill and smooths its surface against his thigh. Once the note is flat again, he starts folding its long edge, inch after inch. The note takes the shape of an accordion. He places it on top of the two beer bottles, like a bridge. Carefully, he balances the third bottle on top of the bridge. Then he lets go. The bottle stands on top.

The girl scoffs and looks away. "Whatever. That's a lame trick. And who buys a girl a *beer* anyway?"

Too distracted by the news Laura has brought him, Dennis doesn't reply. The girl stares at the beer bottle, sitting on top of the bill. For a while, they're both lost in their own thoughts.

Solomon must have a reason for not using the override protocol. It's long overdue, especially after the financial hit they took in City of England when project Kinship went down. After the cruise ship in the port at City of Serbia got away, with a crew of rebels that not only stole a CS-key from the Chip-Center, but one of the capsuled test subjects as well. But most of all, the rebels had somehow managed to wipe out a fortune in CC's from numerous Chip-Charity accounts. Kaarina, William, and their following were all supposed to die. Out there, without them having to spend any more city resources or funding. Gunned down on the street, starved to death, torn apart by wildlife… the odds were never in their favor. But now, the Unchipped have turned the city's own against them. And not just anybody, but one of the *founders*. A mastermind like Margaret.

Why isn't Laura taking action already?

"Okay, old man. You're starting to act like a train wreck here. And I'm not sure I'm your station."

Dennis looks up, surprised. Too bad she's so young. The girl's got some spunk after all. Her gaze starts to wander curiously around the SIM-bar, but Dennis fails to care. He can't let go of the mystery that is Laura Solomon's mind. He rubs his face, suddenly tired of playing these games. A long exhale escapes his lips. "What could be so important..." he mumbles.

Orange-lips tilts her head, refocusing on the man sitting in front of her. "What's that?"

Dennis drops his hands onto his lap and shrugs. "Let's say you are the world's most powerful woman," he says. The girl's chin rises an inch. Her young arrogance likes this game. "And you could fix a problem by pressing a button. One click and boom, you're back on track. Ruling the world. Saving humanity."

"But?"

"But something's holding you back. Not something—*someone*. You want to protect them more than anything else. So, who are you protecting?"

"Am I married?"

"Single. Married to your career."

"Do I have friends?"

Dennis considers this. Is he Laura's friend? She did

call him on his birthday. Gave him a present. She remembered his likes and habits. Called him 'Texas.' Is that what friends do?

"Well?"

"No, you don't have any friends. Only colleagues and employees."

"But I have someone out there that I need to protect?"

Dennis nods. "Yes. But who?"

Her orange lips turn into a half-smile. "Well, that's easy. Any woman, no matter how powerful or isolated, will always protect her children."

Dennis's head snaps back. Children? Laura's?

"That's highly unlikely. Remember, you're not married."

The girl leans back in her chair and laughs wholeheartedly. "Who is, these days? It doesn't mean children don't happen. Made in the lab or not, a kid is a kid. Your blood, flesh, and DNA."

The lab. The Nursery-Center. The puzzle pieces click together while Dennis stares at his companion in shock. Laura Solomon has a child. A daughter or a son. Traveling with the rebels.

He stands up and takes the beer bottle down, sets it on the table. This girl is smart, even if she acts like a brainless maneater. And the way people will underestimate her because of her dumb blond effect could be quite useful to him. Maybe he could save her? Make something out of her? He hands the folded note to the girl and nods. "Send over your CC-account information, doll. You just earned yourself a butt-load of funds and a job."

She takes the hundred-dollar bill, taps on her AR-glasses, swipes the air, and then looks at Dennis. "A job, huh?" She gets up and fixes her short dress, nodding at the toilet door in the distance. "Is that what your generation calls it?"

Without leaving the scene, Dennis accesses his account and sends a thousand CC's to the account number he just received. Then he reaches for his glasses, suddenly wide awake.

"We need to track a kid. First thing tomorrow morning."

"A kid?"

"I'll have my people send you the address. Take the elevator to the fifteenth floor. Eight a.m. sharp. Don't be late."

"And which apartment is it?"

"The only one on that floor. You can't miss it."

"And who do I ask for? An old man who likes to trick eighteen-year-old girls and buy them beer?"

Eighteen. Christ. He really dodged a bullet there.

"Sure. Ask for a man who'd rather see that eighteen-year-old kid work to save the world. Instead of spending her time at SIM-bars trying to earn a quick buck."

Something dark passes across her face. Embarrassment? Regret? Then she stands up, nods at Dennis. "I'll be there. Eight a.m.."

19

"Good. And to answer your question, ask for Dennis Jenkins." He lifts his hand to leave the bar. "But my friends call me Texas."

5

THE RESORT

March 2089
Iceland

5

THE RESORT

March 2089
Iceland

CHAPTER 1
KAARINA

The cold breeze plays with the silk curtains. Cool air pushes its way across the hotel room, sending goosebumps over Kaarina's naked body. Weeks, almost a month. That's how long it's been since she stepped off the cruise ship and got to sleep on solid ground again. No more seasickness. No more restless nights, filled with nightmares of drowning. Or that's what she had thought. Here she lies, though, wide awake and anxious again. True, the bed in the hotel is as steady and sturdy as it should be, but each time she closes her eyes, the mattress starts swaying.

A faint nickering sound reaches Kaarina's ears through the open window. The lamp in the courtyard casts its light onto the wall, a bright spot surrounded by the long shadows of the silk curtains. She picked the room right beside the resort's horse stables. Not that the horses live in the stalls anymore. They moved out of the barnyard a long time ago. But now they hear people again. The clanking of pots and plates while breakfast is being made. Kids running around the pool deck. People walking on the paths between the hotel and the small village with its endless cottages. Just like other wild animals, like rabbits, minks, and reindeer, the horses now come around, looking for carrots and oats and flakes of hay. Kaarina gives them what she can find, though most of the grain sacks and hay bales in the storage room are covered in mold.

The mattress squeaks under her weight. The man next to her turns on his side but doesn't wake up. His back and buttocks are only partly covered by a thin white sheet. A murmur. Grunting. He's sound asleep, utterly oblivious to both Kaarina's muddled state of mind and their agreement. He's supposed to sneak out and return to his own room—right after. Maybe it was just an accident that he fell asleep. Or maybe he chose to forget their agreement, just as Kaarina now pretends to be bothered by the fact that he's still here.

Carefully, one leg at a time, she gets out of bed. She reaches down to the floor for the three-sizes-too-large bathrobe. Her footsteps soft and cautious, Kaarina walks to the open window and sits on the writing desk right underneath. The fresh air helps with her ghostly seasickness, but it also keeps her awake at night. She leans out the window, trying to take a peek at the barnyard. A shadow moves in the night, hoof steps echoing on the concrete in front of the outdoor stalls.

It should feel like home. This. The horses. A solid,

normal bed. People. A community. It should feel like winning a war—against all odds.

They've escaped. Again.

They've outsmarted the Chipped. Again.

Kaarina should be happy-dancing. Grinning. Beaming. Or like they said back when religion was still a thing, and people believed in gods and spirits instead of rabbits' feet and sacred rocks:

I should count my blessings.

But none of that has happened. No happily leaping around her safe new home. No laughter by the poolside, hugging her new family members. Her friends and allies. No, instead, she's fallen into a self-destructive pattern; moping and snapping. Lashing out. Sneaking around in the night. With a man who could do so much better. Not that she'd ever tell him that. He doesn't need to know she cares.

She pulls the window shut, leaving the wild horses to their treasure hunt. Her bare feet slapping against the floor, she makes her way to a hefty gaming chair at the furthest corner of the room. A chair for the Chipped. Something she's seen in the cities; a throne. One that doesn't belong to Kaarina, but her enemy. Regardless of whether she's won the war or not.

But has she won? Really? Fleeing and escaping is hardly winning. People look at her and see a fearless rebel leader.

All she sees is a coward.

Kaarina sits down, her fingers trailing along the

gaming chair's soft leather. Her gaze scans the room, skipping the naked, snoring man. She stares at her backpack under the bed. A laptop and a memory stick rest inside. Forgotten. Seemingly useless. Just like Kaarina and the people she's brought to live with her here in a remote, abandoned Chipped resort.

"You can't get away with this…" Her whisper hisses in the dark room. As she closes her eyes, the images flash through her tired mind.

Friendly but piercing eyes.

A sincere-looking but deceptive smile.

A face, an expression that says, "Let me help. You're nothing without me."

A white lab coat, floating in the wind by a stone wall with carvings.

A pair of sensible shoes, thumping against the ground of Kaarina's home country—a place she can never return to.

"You *won't* get away," she whisper-hisses again. "Because I won't let you." Her nails dig into the armrests, damaging the elegant leather. "I'll stop you, Laura Solomon. If it's the last thing I do."

Fiddling and poking at the empty hay nets, the bay horse moves closer across the barnyard. Kaarina wrinkles a wrapper in her hand; a soft peppermint candy. Her eyes follow the gelding's every movement. She takes deep breaths, inhaling the heady smell of moldy hay, shavings, and manure. She can't help but close her eyes, still crinkling the candy wrapper in her hand.

Here, with eyes shut and no one around, Kaarina feels at home. Like she never left the hayloft in a horse barn by the suburbs, near City of Finland's blue lights and high stone walls. A city where her mother's house still stands, as does her old apartment. Those homes are now occupied by Finns whose brains had accepted Solomon's computer chip and integrated with her program. Those rooms are not for a girl like Kaarina, with a malfunctioning chip and enough bad luck for a lifetime.

Back there, her life no longer exists. The horses, cats, deer, and raccoon-dogs. Kaarina used to be one of them. A creature of the forest. An animal, at ease with the fact that the world had come to its end. All was well.

But then, the what-if games became an everyday thing. What if she could be a part of Laura Solomon's new world after all? What if she could do better?

And then, Laura Solomon had promised her a quick fix, doubling her lust and curiosity for the life that had been denied her. Growing her false need for more. Her greed. A desire for something convenient, maybe even luxury. A new life in the city. She had wanted to belong, to be part of a community. And Solomon had read her mind, understanding her almost as well as one of the Unchipped would have. "Feed me!" Kaarina had screamed, without ever opening her mouth. "Accept me as one of you! Teach me to fly!"

The peppermint digs into her palm as Kaarina makes a fist. Tears of rage push through her closed eyelids. If only she hadn't listened… If she had realized sooner what Solomon and the Happiness-Program were all about, she could have simply left the suburbs of the blue city without drawing any attention to herself. But no. Now, she and her little clan of rebels are on the Solomon Foundation's most wanted list. Then again, if events had played out differently, she might never have met these people—her friends—and some of them would surely be in stasis capsules by now.

Something soft nudges her white-knuckled fist. Kaarina opens her eyes. A smooth muzzle pushes against her hand, whiskers ticking the back of her palm. She fingers the candy wrapper open and lays the treat in the middle of her open palm. A big, soft lip takes the treat.

"Good fella," she whispers. A short laugh escapes her throat. She extends her hand and pets the long, fluffed hair on the horse's neck. "My name is Kaarina," she mumbles to her new friend. Then she shakes her head. "But who needs names anyway. You, my friend… you're too good to be labeled like that. You don't need a name. You're free. No locked stall doors for you. No window bars. You'll never wear another halter or bridle. You go as you please…"

"Sorry to interrupt. But can a William join this Anarchists Anonymous meeting?"

Kaarina can't see Bill, but she senses him tapping her

from somewhere nearby. He probably doesn't want to startle Kaarina's new equine friend.

Don't walk straight behind him. Let him know you're coming. No sudden movements, either.

A low chuckle, somewhere behind Kaarina's back. With steady, calm steps Bill approaches the horse. He extends his hand and caresses the long, tangled mane. "Whoa. She's something else."

"He."

"How do you know?" Bill asks, turning slightly toward Kaarina, but keeping his eyes on the majestic animal right beside him.

"Horse junk? That's what you came here to talk about?"

Bill takes a step back and folds in half to peek under the animal's stomach. Then he gets up and continues stroking the horse from its withers. "I think you're mistaken. Zero balls down there, Kay."

Kaarina can't help but smile. For a fleeting moment, she's distracted from stasis capsules, brain chips, rebel armies, and Laura Solomon's lab attire. "It's a gelding, not a stallion." Kaarina gets up and scratches the horse under his mane.

"Must be shitty," Bill says, staring at the horse.

"What is?"

"Getting snipped."

Kaarina huffs, then continues scratching the gelding's neck. Though her best friend has created a welcome distraction, muddled thoughts rush back in—and then right out—her tired brain. She can't remember a time when she felt this disoriented. Lost. Angry.

"Look," Bill whispers, pointing at a stained gray horse standing near a rotting round hay bale.

Kaarina crinkles the candy wrapper in her hand. The gelding next to her nickers, but doesn't search her for more treats. Instead, he turns around and walks to his equine friend. Together they disappear behind the barn.

Bill sits down on the concrete mounting block in the middle of the yard. Kaarina shoves her hands into her pockets and investigates her friend's face. "How's it going today?"

Bill looks up and shrugs. "Slept in. Found more booze in the basement storage. This place has more alcohol than City of California and City of England combined."

Kaarina scoffs and turns her face to hide her smile. She sits down next to Bill.

"And you?" he asks her.

"So far, so good. The kids seem to like this place, and everyone's pretty happy here. Or as happy as they can be under the circumstances. The Chipped don't seem to care how little we have. They don't seem to miss the city one bit."

Bill's shoulder brushes against hers. "No, Kay-Kay. I asked how *you're* doing."

"Me?"

"What, has the ocean air frozen your malfunctioning brain?" Bill turns and knocks his knuckles against

Kaarina's head a tad too hard. "Yes, *you*. What's going on in that blond head of yours?"

Kaarina hugs her legs against her chest. She closes her eyes and pretends that she's sitting on a fallen, moss-covered tree trunk, deep in the woods of her homeland. The place where she grew up, the place she never thought she'd leave. Old trees and murky skies. Tall grass and eerie silence. She can almost hear the hedgehogs and raccoon-dogs crawl out from their nests under tree roots and the ruins of buildings. Sniffing for food, they roam the ditches and rocks. It's a new, better world for them. Nature's biggest predator doesn't come around anymore.

"Kay?"

She shakes her head and opens her eyes. "I'm... I don't..." But the words stick in her throat.

"Go on." His face is serious now. He's been waiting for this moment, for Kaarina to open up to him like she tends to do, because he knows her mind as well as anyone.

She inhales sharply. "I don't know what to do."

"About what?"

"About any of it." Under her brows, she glances at Bill, then looks down at the ground again. "I feel like I've failed everyone."

"Why's that?"

"Why?" She huffs and gives him a dry laugh. "This war would have never happened without me. If I had been smart enough back then... If I had listened to you, if I had just stopped to think, just for a fucking moment, maybe I wouldn't have gone back to her to get my brain poked and hijacked."

"Solomon? You're talking about the Chip-Center? What happened in City of Finland?"

"What else?"

"Hm."

"Bill, I started this whole mess. Me. If I had never talked to Markus..." her voice breaks and her throat is suddenly too swollen for her to keep going.

"Hm." Bill thinks for a while. Then a genuine smile spreads over his face. "You know... It's not exactly your responsibility alone to save the world and the people in it."

"No?"

"No."

"But our people look to me for leadership and it's a lot of pressure. I'm always worried I'm making the wrong decisions and that they'll pay the price. So, yeah, it's definitely my job to save the world. If not me, then whose job is it?"

Bill grins briefly, then pretends to think hard while he rubs his jaw, which is covered by a three-day beard. "Oh, it's definitely Micky's job to save the world. He seems to know enough to do so. Actually, he seems to know it all. What I should eat, and wear, and say..."

She looks up at Bill and gives him a wry smile. Having something so ordinary as a relationship issue to think about is just what Kaarina needed. And it's clear

Bill knows it, too. "Say it isn't so," she teases. "Trouble in paradise?"

"It's not so much trouble," he says, giving Kaarina a smile, "as it is me wanting to go live alone in a cave, or just have a drink with someone who doesn't talk all the time. Like Yeti."

"Wow."

"I know, I know." Bill sighs and takes a moment to fix his dreadlocks into a neat bundle that rests against the back of his neck. "It's just living in a small hotel room together, spending all our time glued to each other's side. Eating, drinking, sleeping, taking walks together day in and day out…"

"Sounds to me like you need some alone time, friend."

His eyes narrow. "But isn't that kind of a fucked-up thing to want? When all we have left now is each other?"

Kaarina can't help it; a jaw-stretching yawn escapes her mouth.

"Oh, excuse me! Am I *boring* your rebel ass?"

She smiles and can't help another yawn. "No, no. It's not that. I'm just tired, I guess. I haven't been sleeping that well."

"Oh. Oh, fun," Bill says with a sarcastic tone. "A guessing game. Let's see, what's keeping world-renowned rebel leader Kay-Kay awake at night?" He pauses and taps the tips of his fingers together. "Kay-Kay can't sleep because… Hmm, could it be the fact that the world as we know it has come to its end?" He pretends to wave the thought off as ridiculous. "No, that's old news. How about the fact that we could be attacked at any given moment? Possibly murdered in our sleep?"

"Thanks, Bill. You've really cheered me up here."

"Humanity destroying itself? Lack of Mexican cuisine in this joint? The dogs liking me better than you?"

"Mm." Kaarina nods repeatedly. "Ässä *has* been spending an awful lot of time in your room."

"And don't forget the expiring firewalls in our Chipped friends' heads! That's worth a sleepless night or two." Kaarina nods again, this time her smile fading. Their little theater for two is starting to feel more like a tragedy than a comedy.

Bill picks up on her darkening mood and waves her off. "Hey, I'm just messing with you. If Solomon's crew was able to attack us, she would have been all over that a long time ago. Besides, Ava's theory that Margaret has somehow hacked our people's chips and installed firewalls is growing on me. Though I would hope that Luna could confirm it by doing the same."

"Right. It's just that—Ava's theory."

"Yeah, well. The kid knows this genius way better than any of us. And so far, she's been right. We're safe here."

Kaarina clears her throat. "How's the CC collection coming?" she asks, eager to change the subject.

"Luna has my CS-key," Bill says. "She's on it." He

crosses his legs and cups his hands around his knees. "A few more days, and we'll have more money than the black market has supply."

Kaarina stands and takes a carpet knife from her pocket, then walks to the round hay bale. Running the blade on the white plastic that covers the bale, she circles it. Then she slices the white plastic into three even pieces. Yellow, partly brown hay pokes out from its prison.

Bill gets up and walks over. "Is it good for them to eat?" he asks.

Kaarina reaches for a handful of straw and takes a sniff. Flustered, she tosses it on the ground and stomps on it. "Moldy as fuck."

"Well, hey," Bill says and hovers his hand above Kaarina's shoulder. Their friendship is more the punching kind than the hugging kind. "We'll figure it out. It's only been three weeks."

"Three and a half," Kaarina says. She folds the blade back into the knife and shoves it into her pocket.

"I'm going out to draw today," Bill says. "Just about to leave. Maybe I'll find some hay and bring it back?"

Kaarina waves him off. "Don't bother. If there's hay out there, the horses will find it. They don't need me." *None of the animals do anymore,* she adds in her mind.

Bill gives her a long look, which she dodges. Then he pulls out a stack of papers and a pencil. He nods toward the open field that leads to the small village by the resort. This is where most of their people now live.

A row of rusty-looking speakers encircles the cottages, casting their shade on the dry ground. Old outdoor warning sirens, with matching smaller speakers in each room inside the hotel. In case of an Emergency. That's what the security leaflet at the hotel lobby taught them when they first arrived.

"Why don't you come with me today?"

"No thanks. You're the graphic designer. Not me."

"I could use a fresh set of eyes."

Kaarina rubs her eyes, then her whole face. She wishes she could shake the feeling that she's about to crash at any given moment.

She turns to hide her teary eyes, walking away. "Just get it done," she says. "Draw your damn Unchipped-World so we can hide from the world like cowards and rot away in the rain like that moldy hay bale."

Bill frowns and stares after her.

"Is it the hotel?" he yells after her. "Is that what's really bothering you?"

Kaarina stops but doesn't turn around to face Bill. "What about the hotel?"

"You know what I mean."

"You mean the basement."

"I know you don't want to talk about it. But it's like a big fucking pink moose in the middle of the room, waving its horns at us, begging us to notice its ugly mug."

"Antlers."

"Whatever, Kay. It needs your attention."

Squeezing the carpet knife in her pocket, Kaarina closes her eyes. Tears roll down, and she lets them. Instead of the memory of forest animals and the smell of a horse barn, different kinds of sensations flow in and fill her mind.

White pills shaped like American footballs, scattered around the bathroom floor.

Her panicked footsteps on neon-blue tiles.

White lab shoes. Following her, no matter where she goes.

Without a word, she walks on.

"Don't just stroll away like a teenager with an attitude!"

"Fuck you, Bill."

"Fuck me? Kay, this is not you. I'm just trying to help! We all are!"

But you can't help me, she thinks, her sneakers pausing on the ground. How could anyone help her, when all she wants is to see Doctor Solomon suffer? To see her pay for what she's done? How is Bill to help her when she's more than ready to sink to Laura Solomon's level? To get even. To get revenge.

"Talk to me, Kay!"

Kaarina kicks a small rock on the ground. It jumps against the concrete and rolls under a stall door. "I don't know Bill. How could I know? Why should it be me who makes the decisions?"

"Like I said, you don't have to decide anything alone. We've all seen the basement. It makes us all sick.

But Kay, people look up to you. Like it or not—and I know you don't—you are their leader."

"Yeti's the fucking leader."

"Yeah, well," Bill hesitates to continue. "Not to all of us."

Kaarina lowers her chin. More tears stream down her face. She knows Bill can tell, no matter how much she tries to hide them. With a quick swipe, she dries her eyes on her sleeves. "The stasis capsules stay on. We're not touching them." She stands taller, clears her throat. "It's Solomon who's responsible for storing people in those death-pods. Not us."

A lonely chair stands in the middle of the hotel's kitchen floor, facing away from the cooking area. Markus walks over and straddles the seat. He leans his arms on the chair's back, rests his chin on top of his folded hands. With his head tilted, he stares at the industrial oven in front of him.

Kaarina's knuckles brush softly against the entryway's wall, but Markus is too focused on the oven to notice. The divine smell of *pulla* floats around the kitchen. The thought of sweet pastries comforts her, but not because she's hungry: the smell reminds her of her mother.

Afraid she might start crying again, Kaarina tries to shake off the images of her childhood. She knocks again, this time louder. Markus snaps out of his reverie. His deep blue eyes find Kaarina and a warm smile spreads across his face. "Guess what I baked?"

Kaarina walks in, chuckling softly. "Hmm, this is a tricky one." She walks to the cupboards and leans against the counter. She rubs her chin, pretending to think hard. "Oven-sausage? Meatballs? Oh, oh, is it *karjalanpiirakka*?"

Markus laughs and waves her off. "That's it, smart-ass. No *pulla* for you." He rests his chin on his hands again and continues to stare at the rising dough through the oven's glass door. Kaarina turns and opens cupboard doors until she finds the plastic mugs. She takes out two. Then she walks to one of the humongous refrigerators and takes out a gallon of soy powder milk. They should be more sparing, since it's not clear when they'll be able order more from the black market. But right now, she's too tired to focus on shoulds and should nots. She pours the milk and walks over to Markus. He takes the mug from her and nods at a chair by the kitchen table.

After fetching a chair, Kaarina sits down next to him, mirroring his posture. In silence, they stare at the pastries, taking small sips of cold milk. Heat reflects on their faces, leaving their skin flushed and warm. A small smile is stuck on Markus' face as he rests his cheek on his folded hands, turning now to stare at Kaarina. She squirms under his gaze. Nervous, she laughs a little, dodging Markus' unusually bold stare. "What? Don't tell me I have a milk-mustache?"

His smile deepens. "No, it's not that. I mean, sure, that mustache of yours would make Yeti himself jealous. But that's not it."

Kaarina wipes her upper lip clean. "What then?" She smiles back at him, the man who once saved her life.

"I'm really proud of you."

Kaarina huffs. She turns her gaze back to the oven. "Don't be silly."

"No, really. It was you who brought us here. To safety. All those people, the kids... thanks to you, they now have a home and good people around them. Plenty of food and water."

"Shit-tons of *pulla* can't be considered plenty of food, Markus."

But he doesn't joke back. Just smiles and stares. After a minute of silence, he says, "I wish you could see yourself the way I see you."

"Which is what? A dirty barn girl?"

"Intelligent. Brave. A unique person."

Kaarina huffs again and buries her face into her folded arms. The back of the chair digs into her forehead. "It's normal for the Chipped to be fascinated by the Unchipped," she mumbles. "Opposites attract."

Markus doesn't say anything. She knows he hates being labeled like that. Hates that people are categorized by the status of their brain implant. He gulps down the rest of his milk and sets the mug on the floor next to his chair. Then Markus gets up, grabs a kitchen towel, and opens the oven. When he pulls out a sheet of golden-brown sweet buns, Kaarina pushes her nose against her hoodie sleeve. The longing for her mother makes her feel like she's five years old again.

"This batch came out really good. The last sheet got burned. I guess I misjudged the egg powder to milk ratio…" Markus's voice fades out as Kaarina's restless thoughts consume her. She thinks of her mother, dead on the bathroom tiles. Her father, who walked out on them and never came back. Is he Chipped? Chipless? Dead?

If Kaarina hadn't been so eager to live the carefree, convenient life City of Finland had offered her, maybe she could have stopped the war from happening. If she had just laid low, stayed in the barn in the middle of the woods. If she hadn't pushed her luck, visited the city, met Markus…

No. No, no, no. It's *not* Kaarina's fault. It's *hers*. The evil Finnish witch in a white lab coat and good shoes. Shoes that she uses to crush anyone who dares to stand in her way. Anyone small, insignificant, meaningless. At least in *her* eyes. Those who don't fit the great Laura Solomon's plans for a new and better world.

"…and obviously there's no cardamom in the mix either—"

"Markus, I want to destroy her."

Markus looks up from the pastries. "Who? What now?"

Kaarina looks up, her forehead aching from pressing against the chair. "Solomon. I want her gone. Or if I can't get rid of her, I want to make her pay at least. For everything she's done."

Markus drops the bun he's holding. With a faint

thump, it lands back on the baking sheet. "Kaarina, hey…" He takes a few steps toward her, then freezes. His smile is gone, and a frown shadows his kind eyes. "Where's this coming from? Why are you bringing this up now? I thought you just wanted us all safe. That you didn't care about the past."

She tries to look stern and ignore the fact that her hands have begun to shake. "I did. I still do. But Solomon put those people down there. In those capsules. She put them there and left them to rot. We need to get those people out of there. What if that was one of us there? Owena or Sanna?"

Markus gasps, his eyes wide. "Hey, no need to bring the kids into this scenario. Stop painting the devil on a wall."

"You stop with the idiotic Finnish sayings."

Markus spreads his hands, helpless before her stubbornness. He reaches for the chair, leaning his hands on its back again, but he doesn't sit down. Blue eyes drill into Kaarina's, filled with worry. "So you want to finish the Happiness-Program for good."

Kaarina nods.

"What is it exactly you're planning to do?"

"I want to free the people in the capsules."

"The four downstairs?"

"No. Everyone."

"Kaarina, that's—"

"We need to stop Solomon from turning people into mindless machines."

Markus's lips press into a line. He doesn't look at Kaarina, but she knows she has his full attention.

"If we can figure out how to get these people out here, we can get anyone out. Even those who are stuck in the Chip-Centers around the world. It's up to us now, Markus. And I know it's just the few of us here, but maybe we can find more people to join—"

"I'm sorry to interrupt you, but what about Sloboda? We took her out. And now she's fighting for her life."

"I know she is, Markus. But she was sick when she first went in. Luna thought she was dead. And how were we to know she would just go and open the capsule like that and drag Sloboda out of there?"

"But we don't know what makes her so ill. It may have been us unplugging her, just as well as it may have been her sickness."

"That's exactly why we need to figure it out. All of it. How to open the capsules. The rest of the Chipped technology. Details of Doctor Solomon's operation. Everything."

"And what if touching the capsules will alert Doctor Solomon? And then she'll know that we're here?"

"Well…" Kaarina clears her throat. She hasn't thought this through. But she needs this goal. A plan. Action is the only thing that makes her feel strong and confident. She's done feeling weak and helpless. "We'll need to do some research before we do anything else."

"I just…" Markus sucks in his lower lip. It's hard for him to argue with Kaarina. With anyone really, but especially her. And she hates how she's now using it against him. But she needs an ally.

"I'm not saying we should go unplug everyone from the capsules and see what happens. I think it's essential we keep them safe until we find out how the computer system works."

Markus exhales and nods. "Good. Okay."

Kaarina gets up from the chair and folds her arms. "To do that, we need more information. We need to hack Solomon. Think about it. We have Margaret's computer. Two CS-keys. We've got Luna, who's the next best hacker we could wish for, after losing Margaret."

Markus nods. "She's been teaching some of the kids computer skills, and some of the people are quite tech savvy. It's not much right now, but maybe in a year or two—"

"We can't wait that long. Luna will be fine, we'll help her as much as we can. With just the right information, we can attack Solomon without her ever finding out what hit her. If we had access to her computer, we could do so much more than just ruin her capsules."

Markus winces. "More? You mean—"

"Let's not get ahead of ourselves. All I'm saying is that we shouldn't duck our heads like a bunch of cowards. Why is it that we're always yielding? Always being the bigger person?"

Markus watches Kaarina's eyes. He waits a long

time, hesitating. His Adam's apple moves up and down as he swallows. "And what does Yeti say about this?"

Kaarina blinks rapidly. "Yeti?"

"Yeah. Does he approve of this plan?"

Kaarina lifts her chin. "I wouldn't know," she says. "Because Yeti doesn't know anything about this. I came to you first."

Markus stares at her, holding his breath. For a moment of silence, he exhales and lowers his gaze. "You know I'll help you, Kaarina. I always will. But could we take a step back and think about this? Really, think about the consequences. It's not just you and me. It's hundreds of lives. Is revenge really more important than the safety that this place brings? The second chance we all have here?"

"Prisons can be safe, sure."

"I don't understand. What are you trying to say?"

"What about freedom?"

Markus sits down on his chair. He leans his head against his hands, keeping his eyes on Kaarina. "You really want to go after that lunatic?"

Kaarina moves her chair closer to Markus's and sits down. She takes his hands between hers and looks deep into his eyes. "If I don't go after her... who the hell will?"

Green mountains rise behind the graveyard. Long grass, weeds, and debris swirl in the wind. Sunlight finds brief openings as the clouds pass by, throwing long shadows across the gravestones. Kaarina stands behind the crowd, staring at Luna, kneeling by the hole in the ground where Sloboda now lies. A yellow dog sits next to her, pressing against Luna's slightly shaking body.

Owena and Sanna stand with Niina—a Chipped woman from City of Finland. Ever since they disembarked from the boat, Niina's spent all her time looking after the two girls. Her protectiveness seems odd to Kaarina, bordering on obsession. Especially because these days, Niina doesn't seem that interested in her own daughter Ava's well-being. "Whatever," the Unchipped girl just says, whenever Kaarina tries to ask her about her mother's odd behavior.

Bill stands right behind Luna, holding her coat. A chilly breeze sends goosebumps over Kaarina's arms. Cold sweat trails down her ribcage under her oversized T-shirt. Did she do this? Is she responsible? She could have guessed it wasn't safe to unplug Sloboda from her capsule. Luna would have listened, back in City of Serbia. Yeti too.

"Hey, if anyone's responsible, it's me." Yeti's low voice echoes through her scattered mind. *"I'm the one who carried Sloboda out of there."*

Kaarina looks up at the sky, blinking rapidly. The clouds are getting thicker, darker. She fights the tears but lets her anger flush through her body. *I thought we agreed not to tap each other here.*

"Yeah, well." There's a short pause before Yeti

46

continues their silent conversation. *"That's not the only agreement that we've broken."*

Blond hair on his broad chest, trailing down toward his navel. His lips on hers, his arms wrapped around her slightly shaking hips, his fingers digging into the back of her neck… the images flash through Kaarina's mind before she can stop them. Yeti's seen them too. Last night and now again, in her memories. But he doesn't mock Kaarina, doesn't tease. They stand and stare at Luna's back, not talking but still connected.

People around them start gathering the kids, turning back toward the previously abandoned village they now call *home*. Markus picks up Owena, who wraps her arms around his neck. The little girl waves at Kaarina as they pass. Kaarina waves back, giving Markus an uncertain smile. He nods at her in return.

Bill sets Luna's coat on her shoulders and sits by her, silently. The yellow dog gets up to wag his tail, but then sits back down and leans against his grief-stricken master. They aren't talking, Luna and Bill, not silently or out loud. Luna's lost in her sorrow, staring into the dark pit where her friend now rests. Would she agree with Kaarina's plan? She doesn't know the Serbian girl well enough to say.

"Plan? What's the plan, Kid?"

Don't call me that.

"What the fuck is the plan, Kaarina?"

Yeti's tone has changed. He's once again the fearless Unchipped leader. The protector and problem-solving

47

warrior, who would walk through fire and lava for his people. Kaarina envies the way people look at him. Envies his steady, calm way of taking over the room whenever he talks. It annoys her more than Bill's dramatic outbursts or how Markus never loses his temper. Not even when provoked—when it would be the sensible thing to do.

Yeti turns and makes his way over. It's just the four of them now, plus the dogs. Everyone else heads back to the village and the small cottages they've made their homes. Markus will head back to the hotel, feed the kids, and comfort the adults. They'll gather around the kitchen table, and later on around a bonfire. They'll chitchat, tell stories, and laugh at each other's jokes until they feel better again. Markus has even managed to get Ava to open up a little. Kaarina's noticed the two spend more and more time together.

Yeti stops and stands an inch too close to Kaarina. His breath tickles her forehead. She wants to fold and take a step back, but she forces herself to look up and face him.

"Spit it out."

"And if I don't?"

"I'll pick your ass up and shake it out of you."

Kaarina looks past Yeti to see if Bill's picking up the tension. But he's still sitting there, wordlessly comforting Luna by the grave.

"You're not touching the capsules," Yeti says, lowering his voice.

"I'm not."

"Don't lie to me."

"I wouldn't," Kaarina lies.

"Bullshit. Do I need to remind you that I practically live inside your head? Just spit it out. Why are we suddenly opening the pods? What's going on?"

She can't help herself. Laura Solomon's face flashes through her mind. Images of the place where she and Yeti once lived, side by side but not together. The woods, the suburbs, even the city. Yeti takes a step back, staring at Kaarina with his narrowed eyes.

"I see. You want revenge."

Kaarina folds her arms, peeks at the grave. Bill is now partly turned on his seat in the grass, staring at them. Dodging his questioning look, Kaarina leans in so only Yeti can hear her. Their faces are close enough for their lips to meet. Her heart beats faster, and she's not sure if it's rage, fear, or lust she feels. "I can take Laura Solomon."

"I know you can." His breath feels hot against her cheek. Kaarina breathes faster.

"And there's nothing you can do to stop me."

When his lips press against hers, she doesn't back away. Bill's voice—his squeal-like screams—fill her head, but she blocks the connection in the middle of his hasty sentence. *Oh no girl, you didn't! I knew it! I—"*

When their lips part, the kiss leaves both of them breathless. Kaarina doesn't care about Bill's whooping, or the fact that Luna now gapes at them open-mouthed.

At least one of them is surprised.

Yeti's not startled by them. Or by Kaarina's plan. Nothing can shake his calm, not even the fact that Kaarina wants to go back to war with the Chipped— just as they've successfully escaped it. A small, crooked smile twists his lips.

"What's so funny?"

"You."

"You're laughing at me? I thought you said I could take her."

"I did. And you can," he says. "I just didn't think it would take you this long to get started."

The hotel corridor is lit by a dim yellow light. The solar electric charger keeps the yellow glow going and provides the hotel and the villagers with more power than they need.

Happy squeals echo through the open windows from the empty pool outside. Markus is in the middle of a story. On the other side of the crackling bonfire the kids sit on lounge chairs or by the side of the pool. A woman's soft voice alternates with Markus's. They tell the story together, first in English and then in Spanish. The kids clap their hands, chuckling happily whenever the Abominable Snowman trips on a treasure or ends up eating too much pea soup, his guts rumbling wildly.

Sanna holds something fluffy against her chest. Mr. Bun-Bun, the bunny she's carried with her ever since she escaped the Chip-Center in City of Finland. Owena is glued to her side, petting the critter's long ears. Niina sits next to them, her eyes never leaving the girls.

Kaarina leaves the window. Her soft footsteps take her further into the hotel. She can't remember which hotel room Luna has picked for herself. They've decided to spread out evenly around the hotel; Kaarina, Luna, Yeti, Markus, Ava, Bill, and Micky. It's clear this resort—once owned and run by the Chipped—is abandoned. When they arrived, everything was covered by white sheets and a thick layer of dust and dirt. The pool stood empty. The hotel doors shut but unlocked. Power off. Tiles off as well.

In the basement, only the four stasis capsules—out of several hundred—were still humming, their tenants trapped inside, seemingly nestled in dreamy, peaceful, perpetual sleep. The other capsules stood dark, doors eerily open. Those who live in the village don't know about the basement. Only the seven who live in the hotel do. Waiting. Watching. Trusting Margaret; she would never have sent them to this place if it wasn't safe.

Would she?

Yellow light shines into the hallway from below the door. It's Luna's room. When Bill handed her a bottle of gin from the pool bar, Luna had excused herself from the nightly storytelling and withdrawn into her room.

Kaarina knocks on the door. "Lu? It's me. Kaarina." No answer. "Can I come in?"

She waits, doubting that Luna will agree to her

51

company. Smiling and pleasant, Luna's one of Kaarina's favorite people. Still, she also knows the woman is a force to be reckoned with. Luna's temper has flared up multiple times. Living alone for so long, and then losing everyone she ever cared for has done a number on her nerves. Then again—everyone's on edge. And with good reason.

The last time Luna had snapped was when Micky used Luna's CS-key as a coaster. His cocktail glass shattered against the conference room wall before Micky had a chance to finish his joke about the Chipped swimming in the pool with no water in it.

Kaarina's about to turn around and leave Luna to grieve for Sloboda in peace when the door opens. Luna's swollen eyes meet Kaarina's. She nods for her to come inside. Kaarina walks into a room identical to hers. Luna tosses a pillow on top of something and sits on the bed. The room is dimly lit, and Kaarina doesn't get a good look at the object. A book? A photo frame?

She sits down on the stool by the small writing desk. "How are you holding up?" Kaarina winces at her own words. "Scratch that. What an idiotic question."

Sitting on the bed, Luna hugs her legs against her chest, staring into space. A small smile lingers on her delicate face. "You know what Sloboda means?" she asks, her voice calm and at ease. Has she really understood that her friend is gone now?

"I don't. What does it mean?"

"Freedom."

Kaarina swallows, dodging Luna's red eyes. Even in

the dim light, her pain is evident, and it rips Kaarina apart. She has to grieve Sloboda's death all over again. And Kaarina can't help but feel at least partly responsible for this. If Luna hadn't been forced by Iris to work for the Chipped and locate Kaarina, she would have been spared the whole mess. "I'm so fucking sorry, Lu."

Luna shrugs and huffs. "What for? You didn't do this. *She* did."

Kaarina holds her breath. Maybe it isn't the wrong time to ask for Luna's help. Maybe the timing could not be better. "So you don't blame me for this?" Kaarina asks. "You blame Solomon?"

Luna tilts her head. She reaches for something under the pillow, then stops to think. Then she gets up and walks to the gaming chair at the end of the room. She takes out the CS-key that blinks a purple light. "Sure, Solomon's part of it. But she's not the one who put Sloboda in that death-capsule. Iris did."

Kaarina thinks of the young woman with blue and white hair.

"I forgot about Iris," Kaarina says.

"I didn't."

"You know, maybe we could find a way for you to reach Jovan. Something tells me you could use an old friend right now." Luna glances at the pillow and whatever lies hidden underneath. She doesn't answer. "Or would you rather forget everything that happened in City of Serbia?"

"Belgrade."

"What?"

"City of Serbia is a term for the Chipped. It's Belgrade."

Kaarina investigates Luna's face, trying to figure out if she is losing her mind or just now finding it. "Would you rather forget Belgrade? Or reconnect?"

Luna walks over and hands the CS-key to Kaarina along with two white pills. Pain killers. To help her tolerate the purple light and the pain it creates in her skull. She stares at the pills on her open palm, not wanting to take them but knowing she won't make it if she doesn't.

"Oh, I haven't forgotten anything," Luna says. "But it's not Jovan I want to reconnect with."

The yellow lights in the basement come to life under their footsteps. It's midnight when Luna and Kaarina make their way downstairs with the CS-keys, Margaret's and Kaarina's computers, and a memory stick with a snippet of code and a map of Iceland. They make their way to an area with shelves, drawers, and mountains of supplies.

Kaarina flips the lights on while Luna opens the computers and fires up the CS-keys. The screen on Bill's CS-key flickers numbers and letters. Kaarina nods at the screen. "Can we still collect the CC's while doing this?"

Luna shrugs, reaching for the old-fashioned

computer. She inserts the memory stick into it. "We have more than we need anyway. Bill's going to send in the order next week."

The black market order for food, clothing, building supplies, medicine, and water has been made together with everyone at the resort. After Luna's hack of the Chip-Charity accounts, they could be considered as wealthy as the upper class of Chipped in the cities.

"What if the Chipped audit the CC accounts?" Kaarina asks.

"I'm not sure I follow."

"They must have noticed the leak by now." Kaarina waits for Luna to nod. "What if they find a way to follow the missing CC's? They would find us in a heartbeat."

Luna plops down on the sheet-covered tile floor. Green numbers run across the screen. "I guess it's possible," Luna says. "But unlikely. Think about it. The Chip System is only a few years old. So are the accounts. Hawk's accounts operate on the dark web and she uses multiple untraceable black market servers around the world. If the Chipped can't figure out how the black market handles thousands of off-radar accounts, I'm sure our one or two accounts are pretty damn safe."

Kaarina sits down on the floor next to Luna. She nods at the memory stick inserted into the laptop. "Do you think Margaret's code has something to do with the black market?"

"Anyone operating inside the black market is a free

agent and wouldn't get involved with the Happiness-Program or those who are against it. No, Margaret operates alone." Rubbing her eyes, Luna taps at the memory stick, momentarily lost in thought. "I think it has something to do with the capsules. What was it again, what was it she said?"

"Who, Margaret?"

"Yeah. When she gave you the stick."

"She said to use it once those I trust the most turn against me."

"And where should you install the code?" Kaarina shrugs, telling Luna what she already suspects: she has no idea. "That's what I thought."

"What makes you think the code has to do with the capsules?"

Luna stares at the CS-key, blinking its painful light as it runs the code. "I was able to use some of Margaret's code to access the CS-key's hidden files. I can only spend twenty minutes or so at a time investigating them. The light…" Luna interrupts her explanation when Kaarina nods, rubbing her temples. She knows. She's Unchipped too. "It has something to do with nanotechnology."

Kaarina cocks her head. "Like, nanobots?"

Luna turns to face the laptop. "Nanobots, picobots… something to do with mind mapping. I'm trying to figure it out, but I'm not really educated in this stuff. And I've been too busy collecting CC's so Bill can send in the order to spend time researching."

"I know you've been busy," Kaarina says. "I didn't mean to sound like I didn't appreciate all you're doing for us. Especially after... when Sloboda..."

Luna's fingers freeze on the keyboard. She digs out an inhaler and takes a puff. Ignoring Kaarina's apology, she then says, "I could use some help if I'm honest. Is there anyone among us that would know about stuff like nanobot machine code?"

Kaarina thinks of the people she now lives with. She knows those who have followed her from City of Finland, but only their names and personalities. Same thing with the Unchipped. And the chipless kids they saved from a children's home in City of England. She doesn't remember everyone's skills by heart, but knows what most of them used to do for a living before The Great Affliction. After the mass-deaths, the Chipped had worked for the city as servers, while the Unchipped spent their days hiding in the suburbs where their only job was to survive another day.

"I'll ask around. You're right, you need some help around here."

A small smile twitches on Luna's lips. "Maybe ask Yeti?"

Kaarina turns to grab a bottle of water from the shelf, but mostly to hide her flushed face. "Why him? I'd ask Jaana or Kimmo from City of Finland. The Chipped tend to be more tech-savvy and Kimmo used to work as a game builder or something like that. He's a way better option than a rebel leader who's roamed in the woods killing and stealing for years." The harsh tone of her words surprises them both. Luna recovers first.

"So what did Yeti do for living? Back before the chipping? He screams military to me. That's what made me think of him. They've used nanotechnology to create military goods for decades."

"I don't remember exactly," Kaarina says, playing with the bottle cap. "We don't really talk that much—" Her cheeks flush bright pink. "Okay, stop laughing at me. It's something to do with management."

Luna shakes her head, grinning. "Well, ask him, the next time you… um… see him."

Kaarina sits down and takes a gulp of water, handing Luna a bottle of her own. While Luna opens the cap to drink, Kaarina investigates her friend's face. It was only a matter of time before she brought it up, after seeing the two kiss at the graveyard. Luna twists the cap back on the bottle and grins. "It was always pretty obvious, my friend."

Kaarina opens her mouth to deny it, but her words fail her. The pink on her face turns deep red.

"It's okay," Luna says and smiles. "I was kind of pleased when the kids told me. Markus seemed surprised too. But hey, that's one hell of a way to let off some steam—"

"*Markus* knows?"

"Well, he wonders, at least. Nobody knows for sure. Except for Bill and me."

Markus. Shit. She doesn't know what he is to her,

but the connection between them has been strong ever since the beginning. Whenever Markus is around, Kaarina feels more at ease. Like she's not the anti-Christ after all. Like she's a tiny bit better person.

"Please don't tell anybody. We..." Kaarina bites her lip, shaking her head. "It's just a fling. I've wanted to keep it a secret for a reason."

"Which is?"

"I just need to... put a label on it, I guess. So I can understand it a bit better myself before I have to share it with other people."

Luna regards her for a while, then makes a gesture of sealing her lips. Seeing her smile again is almost worth the embarrassment Kaarina now feels. The smile lingers on Luna's face long after she dives back into the malware and starts doing things Kaarina doesn't understand.

They sit silently, Luna tapping the keyboard, Kaarina letting her work in peace. The basement is quiet, except for the distant humming of the four stasis capsules at the end of the room. It had been Luna's dog Tiny, along with Ässä, who had found the four unconscious tenants inside them, the very first day they had arrived in Iceland. Barking loudly, the terrier and pitbull had circled the pods, until Kaarina followed them to see what the fuss was about.

Seeing the four people—two women and two men—inside the capsules had given her anxiety beyond anything she had gone through over the last several months. The resort had clearly been created by the

Chipped, and had once been occupied by them as well. But it was clear the place has been empty and unused for years. There must be a reason why Margaret sent them here. And as one of the founders of the Happiness-Program, she must have known it was safe.

But then Margaret herself had disappeared.

"Hey, did Ava ever turn over her phone?" Kaarina asks Luna, snapping her out of her flow.

"Huh?"

"Ava. What happened to her smartphone?"

Luna shrugs. "She gave it up for storage, with the charger and other stuff from the boat. It's all locked up in one of the hotel rooms."

"Was she upset?"

"She was. But more so because of her mother. Niina forgot to meet her that day."

Kaarina nods. "It must be tough on her. First, finding her mom, but then she doesn't seem to care about anything but Owena and Sanna."

"I know, I tried to talk to Niina about it…"

"And?"

Luna frowns. "It's like she's not completely there, you know. Like something in her brain is turned off."

"PTSD?"

"Perhaps."

"Do you think Ava's going to get over it?"

"I feel like she's too obsessed about finding Margaret to care. It's almost like she considers Margaret to be her mother now, not Niina."

"And that's why she wanted to keep her phone," Kaarina says, nodding. "In case Margaret is now Chipped and needs a phone to contact us."

"Right." Luna stretches her long legs and arms. After a long yawn, she adds, "Sure would be nice to have Margaret here so I could pick her brain."

"Ava's sure she got away. That she's safe."

Luna crosses her legs again. With her palms behind her back, she supports her weight against the floor. She must be exhausted, Kaarina thinks.

"Ava's a smart kid," Luna says. "I trust her judgment. And it was her who Margaret first gave the access code to."

Kaarina nods. A rapid blinking startles them. Luna turns to look at the screen, where dozens of new windows pop up, revealing text files. She scans the screen, eyes moving rapidly across text, and it takes all Kaarina's willpower not to interrupt her reading to ask what she's found out.

Luna looks up from the screen. But instead of meeting Kaarina's eyes, her gaze scans the dark basement behind her. Then she gets up, grabs the memory stick, and starts running toward the stasis capsules on the other end of the room. Kaarina scrambles up to follow. "Hey, wait!"

Luna lights up yellow tiles as she makes her way down the row of empty capsules. Their doors rest open, revealing how the equipment has been shut down. Stepping on the tiles is like stomping on a minefield.

Staggering pain enters Kaarina's head, then radiates down her spine. Now more than ever she wishes she'd feel as comfortable taking the pain meds as Luna does. Once she gets to the end of the room, where another yellow-tile staircase rises, she finds Luna kneeling down beside one of the stasis capsules.

"Luna, what the hell? What did you find?"

"The stick. It fits."

"Fits where? The capsules?"

"Yeah.

"But why?"

"Not sure exactly." Luna stands up and faces Kaarina again. "But it seems that our four amigos here are special. I think they're stored away for safekeeping."

"What? Why? And by who?"

"Solomon."

"So they're some sort of… I don't know. Assets?"

"More like prisoners."

Luna gets up, the memory stick pressed into her fist. "These people are not here to be used as servers."

"Then why the hell are they here? Are they rebel leaders? Black market bosses?"

"No, I don't think so," Luna says. She pulls out the inhaler and takes a puff. Then she turns to face Kaarina. The yellow light illuminates her face, making her look paler than she is. "I think all these people used to work with Solomon."

"She stuffed her coworkers into pods and left them here to rot? That's the shocking information you found out just now? Solomon's a dick. Her doing something like this shouldn't be that surprising to you."

Luna doesn't reply. She stares at the closest capsule and the person sleeping inside; an older woman, maybe seventy years old with white hair. Her calm, even facial features seem strangely familiar to Kaarina.

"While I looked for instructions on how to open the capsules safely, I accessed the Happiness-Program founders' files, because one of them invented the whole thing." Luna steps up on the capsule's concrete base and places her hand against the tinted glass. The humming seems to become louder. Luna turns to look at Kaarina. "Some of the founders went missing. Years ago."

"And?"

"And I think they were stored down here. In a basement that is supposed to be out of use. A place where none of the Chipped would come looking," Luna says, staring at the old woman inside the capsule. "And I know this one is the founder who invented the capsule. I just opened her file and you'll never believe..." She taps the glass. "This woman is more special to our doctor than all the rest of them together. We can use this against her, I'm sure."

"Why? What's so special about her?"

Luna presses her face against the tinted glass. "This here, my friend, is Doctor Solomon's mother."

CHAPTER 2
WILLIAM

The dry, cracked ground feels hard against Bill's bare feet. Endless mountains and lava fields open up around him as he passes another lagoon. He stops to admire its clear blue water, playing with the thought of stripping off his dress shirt and khaki shorts to jump in. If Micky were here, he'd probably demand that Bill dive in. The thought makes him smile.

Bill lowers his two storage tubes and his duffel bag to the ground. As he sits down, the earth shakes slightly against his palms. Bill looks up and sees a herd of horses galloping by in the distance. He tries to spot the one he's seen in the courtyard with Kaarina, but can't; they all look the same to him from this distance. Majestic, wild, free.

Bill takes the CS-key out of the duffel bag. He looks around to make sure no one has followed him from the hotel or the village.

"Call Hawk. City of California."

CALL INITIATED

While the three white dots on the Chipped computer appear on the screen, Bill opens the storage tubes and pulls out his plans and a small folded drawing board. He sets four lava rocks on the corners of the paper to keep it from rolling back into its tube-shape. Then he picks up his notebook and pencil case. He should work on the hotel redesign today, figure out the last of the construction supplies they'll need in order to finish their forever-home.

"Bill? You okay?"

The woman's worried tone makes Bill smile. He wants to lie and say no. No, I'm not okay. No, I need to come home—immediately.

"I'm alright, Hawk," he hears himself say instead. "How's the chip-free life treating you?"

The woman stays quiet for a while. Bill can almost hear her gray cloud of hair moving around her tanned and wrinkled face. "Oh, it's treating me well. The same as when you last asked me. Two days ago."

"Ahh, you know. I simply can't resist your charm. It's hard to stay away."

Hawk's laughter fills the air. "Careful now. Who's to say I won't tell Micky about your flirtatious ways. Anyone would think you've swapped teams since you left California."

"Oh, don't worry. Grannies have never been my style."

"I'm pleased. Because I'm not looking for a smart-ass gay lover, either."

Both of them fall silent. Smiling, Bill runs the pen across the paper, letting the creative flow take him over.

"Is that paper rustling that I hear?"

"Yes ma'am."

"And the CC account I created for you?"

"Full as can be."

"Well, I'll be damned. Where exactly did you find this hacker of yours?"

"City of Serbia. Her name is Luna. And the best part? She's not stealing from the citizens."

"No?"

"No. She's stealing from the Chip-Charity."

Hawk hums with approval. "Eat your heart out, Robin Hood."

Bill huffs happily, his eyes locked on the paper in front of him. Hawk's soft footsteps rustle against the dead grass as she walks somewhere around the winery, tucked away but near City of California, the Chipped, and the ongoing war.

"How is everybody?" Bill mumbles, more focused on the task at hand than the old woman's answer. "Jada? Abby? Arturo?"

"They're okay," Hawk answers, her tone changing from carefree to reserved.

"Good, good."

She stays quiet, like she's waiting for the next question. Because Bill never calls without asking it.

"And Maria?"

Her sigh is more apologetic than frustrated. "Bill, we've talked about this. She's gone."

"I know she's gone," he says. His hand moves on the paper, changing pencils on the fly. "But it doesn't necessarily mean she's dead. It was all such chaos; I never checked her pulse. Because she was…she was… There's no way of telling whether it was the tranquilizer or—"

"Or the real gun going off. Yes, Bill. I know. We've gone through this a thousand times. I know it's eating you up, thinking about it, but it's not like you had that many options in the moment. You and Micky barely made it out yourselves. Look, I'm doing the best I can to look into it, but because of the turmoil you guys are causing, we need to lie low for now. And that means no investigating trips to the green city."

They fall silent again. The paper in front of him is filling almost on its own, the plans for his new home coming alive in front of his eyes. But his thoughts are not on what he draws. His thoughts are with Hawk as she walks between the rows of dead grape vines. His thoughts are stuck with Maria—the woman who saved his life in the mansion they both used to call home.

"Well, my friend," Hawk says, grunting as she sits down and taps a wooden table in front of her. Bill can almost smell the scent of fish tacos floating up from the pink taco stand by the parking lot. "It's breakfast time. And you know how I hate people who speak with their mouths full."

Bill scoffs, smiling. "Better not be one of those assholes, then."

"Better not." Hawk pauses, as if to consider what she's about to say. "Bill… about the CC's. I need to ask you…"

"Ask me what?"

The line is quiet for a long time. "Never mind," she says. "Just take care of yourself. You're in a good place, Bill."

"If you say so."

"And maybe stop calling me every other day. Who knows what kind of tracking systems the East-Land Chipped have got these days. I don't care if it was Texas who gave you that CS-key. Nobody's stuff is untraceable."

"Fine. Be that way," Bill says, his tone amused.

"You taking your meds?"

Bill stops drawing. His gaze snaps up from the paper to look at the rising mountains around him. Oh, how he hates the question. How he wishes Maria had never told Hawk about his being bipolar. "I am," he says. "Not that it's any of your concern. Unlike back home, I actually need them here. Shit's pretty fucking tense."

"Shit's tense all over the world, Bill. The war leaves everyone vulnerable. It wouldn't be any different if you had stayed. Besides, I think it's good for you to be with the Finns."

"They barely talk. If you ask them a question, they either say 'yes' or 'no.' One of them told me yesterday that 'silence is fun.' And here I thought I was the crazy one."

"More airtime for you, then."

"I just think if I was home... maybe the city would..."

"William. Let go." Her tone is firm. "Let go of Maria. Let go of the past. All that matters is the present—where you are here and now."

He wants to argue, tell Hawk she's wrong. But the words get stuck in his throat. The anger of losing Maria burns the back of his eyes, threatening him with tears that he hasn't let himself shed. If there's a chance that Maria's still alive, crying would mean admitting defeat.

"Let me know when you run out of pills. I'll have Marco send you more."

"Sure will," Bill says, his voice colder than he would prefer.

The CS-key's light turns dull gray. The call has ended.

Bill nudges the computer hastily, sending it sliding down the ledge beside the plans and papers. It stops near one of the lava rocks, only a few feet away from the blue lagoon. He considers going after it, not to save it, but to make sure it drops into the water. But he sits still, staring at its gray light while frustration and anger surge through his body.

He has a job here. An important one, too. He has a new family; Kaarina, the kids, the dogs. Considering the situation the whole world is in, Hawk's right; he's in a good place. He lacks nothing. Even the food is good here. The water pure and safe to drink. He gets to draw again. Make plans that will help people create a place they can call home. Why does he feel so ungrounded? Why can't he live in this moment and enjoy it—just as Hawk suggested?

Sighing deeply, Bill tosses the pencil from his hand. It lands next to the CS-key and rolls down the cracked lava rock that covers the ground. At the edge of the lagoon, it slows on a short tuft of grass. Then it tips and falls into the blue water.

Bill looks down at the paper in front of him. A building rises on it, tall and majestic, with light tones and clear outlines. Balconies. A pool. Out-of-use horse stables. Metal gates, next to a raggedy guard shed.

Bill was supposed to re-imagine this Icelandic resort, an Unchipped village they'll all get to spend the rest of their days in. Design it, order supplies, isolate them from the rest of the world for good.

But instead of a new beginning—he's recreated the mansion.

"How's it coming along, Beau?"

Bill walks into the room, ignoring the question Micky asks every day. Micky—and everyone else living at the resort—wants to see the plans, and to know when they'll be ordering the goods. The supply order is all they need before their lives can begin. A gateway to self-sufficiency.

An image of the mansion—recreated in Bill's notebook—flashes through his mind. Should he tell Micky? About the picture? About his longing for California? His hopes of finding Maria alive, stuffed away in a stasis capsule in a hidden basement? It's all he's been able to think about, ever since Luna and Kaarina found the four poor bastards, capsulated and forgotten downstairs.

"Grumpy much?" Micky stands in front of Bill, shirtless, his hands tucked into his white cotton pockets. He looks like a model from the AR-catalogue Bill used to draw products for. He forces a smile and says, "It's coming along fine. Just ran out of pencils is all." He thinks of himself, tossing a dozen pencils into the blue lagoon, screaming in frustration. "Just a few more details, and we're good to go."

Micky pinches Bill's cheek. "That a boy. Proud of you, Beau. So, you'll never guess what Ava and I cooked today while Markus…" While Micky goes on about his day at the resort, Bill throws himself on the bed. Staring at the ceiling, he thinks of the CC's Luna has gathered on his CS-key and the account Hawk has created for this purpose specifically. The amount grows every day. Would he have enough? Enough for him to travel home?

"Micky, do you have a list of the black market goods? The prices?"

Micky stops waving his hands in the air. He stares at Bill, vividly upset at him for interrupting the story. "You haven't listened to a word I've said. This one's funny, Bill. We got the dogs to play-attack Yeti while he used the outside shower. Wacko stole his towel—"

"Micky. Please."

A deep sigh. Micky's shoulders fall in defeat. Pouting, Micky looks away from Bill. "Sure, I have a list. You do too. It's in the folder on your CS—"

"Does it include travel expenses?" Bill curses silently. He doesn't mean to be this rude to Micky. He adores the man. Micky might be the single reason why he hasn't completely lost his mind over Maria, while escaping the war and settling in Iceland of all places. Micky and his medication. He could manage losing one of them, but not both.

"Travel? Of course it doesn't include travel." Micky's upset tone has turned into a surprised one. "All flights are auctioned these days. I mean, most of the Chipped can't afford to travel anymore. And after the plague in City of England, most places are restricted. Closed borders all around."

"Is City of California one of those places?"

"You want to go back home, Bill? Is that what this is all about?"

Yes.

Bill can't help but blink rapidly, as he tends to do when he's lying. "No. Of course not. I'm just asking."

"Is this about Maria?" A deep frown shades Micky's gorgeous face. "I can't believe we're having this conversation again." He gives Bill a sad smile. "You *know* how much I adored her. Losing her was like losing a limb. Two limbs. But your irrational hope for her surviving the shooting... Beau, are you—"

"Taking my meds?" Bill curses himself for raising his voice. With a softer tone, he continues, "Yes, Micky, I am taking the pills. And this... *feeling* is more than just an illusion or wishful thinking. I mean, you know they don't just kill people. Why would they? The city needs them. It's not that fucking far-fetched that Maria's still out there."

"But still—"

"Okay, could you just please tell me what the hell does a plane ticket cost these days? An arm and a leg? A piece of my cursed brain? What?"

Micky sighs and spreads his hands. His bare feet don't make a sound as he strolls across the floor and sits on the bed next to Bill. "For you to purchase a one-way ticket home—it would cost as much as the final supply order we're about to send in."

Bill extends his hand and runs his fingertips on Micky's silky back. It's not the man's good looks that he has fallen in love with. It's his wit and good heart. The way he cares for everyone—even those who can't see the kindness and love behind Micky's sometimes outrageous and frustrating ways.

"Are the flights really that expensive? Even for just one person?"

Micky nods and turns to take Bill's hand in his. "Now that's just silly talk," he says. He lifts Bill's hand

and presses his lips against the back of his palm. "Because let's face it, Beau. You'd need two tickets." Micky pushes his chest out and points at his naked upper body. "You're a smart man, you would never leave something *this* fabulous behind. Would you, now?"

The next morning, the seven of them meet in the hotel conference room: Bill, Yeti, Luna, Markus, Kaarina, Micky, and Ava. They gather at the round table with steaming mugs of instant coffee. Luna's the only one who has a CS-key in front of her. It's Bill's and not the one they had stolen from City of Serbia. It's the one with the untraceable CC account—now full of money.

Ava being the one who Margaret is most likely to tap—if she's still coming back—has made the girl part of their leadership crew. Yeti has objected vehemently to the girl being so closely involved on numerous occasions, but Markus and Kaarina have stood their ground. Margaret trusted Ava with the memory stick and her code for a reason. Even if they're not sure what that reason is, it doesn't lessen the fact that the girl is an important part of the rebellion.

Luna checks the screen and turns the computer around, so the purple light blinks against the table and not her face. "We now have more than we need. Almost twice as much as we initially agreed upon."

Micky drums his fists against the table. "This is great

news! I say it's time to celebrate, don't you think?"

Ava smiles next to Micky, nodding. "Micky's right. We could definitely use some cheering up around here. I think a pool party is in order."

Micky smirks at her. "No way we'll let you get wasted, kid. Pool party or not."

"Why not? After all I've been through, I should definitely be considered a grown-ass woman around here."

Bill takes a peek at Luna, wondering how she's taking the suggestion of them throwing a party—when the soil on Sloboda's grave is still freshly turned. But the Serbian woman doesn't look upset. She leans back in her chair, waiting for the whooping to pass. Then she exchanges a look with Kaarina.

"Before you run to the poolside and destroy what's left of your liver," Kaarina says, "Luna and I have something we need to tell you." The whooping ends. All eyes flicker between Luna and Kaarina. "It's about the four occupied capsules downstairs. Luna was able to hack into some of the Happiness-Program files. She found personal information about Doctor Solomon, as well as the rest of the founders who created the technology behind the Chip-System."

"And?" Ava asks. "Why do we care about those old farts?"

Kaarina nods at her. "We care because four of the founders are stored right here in Iceland."

Yeti sits taller in his chair. "Those four downstairs

are big chiefs? Not missing people, but the very assholes who are responsible for the capsules in the first place?"

"Yup. Those assholes," Luna says.

Yeti grunts, then pauses to think. "Well, that changes things. In a way, they're responsible for all of this, don't you think?"

"What do you mean?" Luna asks. "You think they shoved themselves in there? Walked in and closed the door?"

"I don't give a shit who put them in there. I don't even care why."

"Do you care about the fact that one of them is Laura Solomon's mother?"

Gasps and murmurs fill the meeting room. Yeti gets up from his chair and begins to pace in front of the wide windows. The pool area outside is filled with playing children.

"Laura's mother, Mrs. Salonen, is the person behind the stasis capsules. I've read through most of her file, but there's a lot more to go. This woman is more powerful and more intelligent than Doctor Solomon ever was."

Bill clears his throat, just as stunned as the rest of the people around the meeting table. "So she's the queen bee, then. Well, fuck! So why would Margaret send us here? Maybe she wasn't trying to help us after all."

Ava jumps to her feet and bangs her fist against the table. "Take that back, Bill," she says. "Take it back immediately."

Yeti stops next to Ava's chair. "I'm sorry to say, kid,

but the Yankee's right." He looks over at Bill and crosses his arms on his broad chest. The man is a mountain. Just as big and intimidating as the ones that rise at the resort's horizon. "We can't trust anybody outside this room." He lifts his hand to stop Ava's objection. "It doesn't mean that Margaret is the enemy. It just means that we don't have time to wait for her anymore. We need to throw Solomon off course before she tracks us." Yeti looks at Kaarina, then at Bill. "If she doesn't already know we're here, that is."

"There's more," Luna says, pulling something out of her pocket. She sets an inhaler, an empty chocolate bar wrapper, and a memory stick on the table. "The memory stick Margaret gave Ava," she says and lifts the small device up for all to see, "It fits the stasis capsules."

"Fits?" Bill says. "You mean it can be inserted into the pod?"

Luna nods. "We think the stick is the key to open the capsules safely…" Luna's voice breaks, and she needs to stop to clear her throat. "Without injuring the person inside. So that whatever happened to Sloboda wouldn't happen to her."

"And what exactly happened to her?" Yeti asks. "Do we even know?"

"I'm not a hundred percent sure. But I've done some research. It seems the capsules may have some sort of, umm…"

"What?" Yeti asks. "Spit it out."

"Healing capacity," Luna says, hesitating.

"Like, curing sicknesses and stuff?" Ava asks.

Micky scratches his head. "That can't be right. All those people, in all those cities... Can they all really be sick?"

Luna opens her mouth but can't find the words.

"What, so Sloboda was cured of cancer in the capsule?" Yeti continues with the questions. "And we basically killed her when we pulled her out?"

Kaarina looks at Luna. When she remains tongue-tied, she speaks for her. "We don't really know. Right now, we have more questions than answers. We'll need to keep reading the files and dig deeper to solve all this. But if the capsules do cure people, it may explain why Doctor Solomon has stored those four downstairs. Maybe they were sick and she's trying to save them. But that's just one theory—"

"Maybe we can wake them up and ask?" Micky says, spreading his hands.

Ava jumps up and takes a sidestep. "Why would we ever wake them up? They're the reason for all of this! The reason we had to run away, the reason Margaret is missing."

"Not just Margaret," Markus adds. "*Millions* of people."

Kaarina leans back in her chair. She runs her hand through her blonde hair. "I know. Trust me, I know." She looks out the window, then cups her face in her hands. "But there must be a reason why Solomon would leave them here. Either she's trying to protect them, heal them, or..."

"By turning them into veggies?" Ava says, huffing. Yeti walks over to her and places his hand on her shoulder. Ava crosses her arms on her chest, won't sit down, but calms down enough to listen what Kaarina has to say.

"Like I said, Laura is either protecting the founders, or something happened between them."

"Such as what?" Markus asks.

"A disagreement," Bill says. "What if they fought against Solomon's plan? Maybe they were against storing people in the capsules and getting everyone chipped."

They all consider Bill's words in silence, Kaarina and Luna nodding at him. They've thought the same thing. Ava's gaze travels between the three of them. She then huffs again, flustered and furious. "You can't be serious. We finally find a safe place. A home. We get enough money to order what we need to become self-sufficient, to isolate ourselves from the Happiness-Program for good… and now you want to wake up the people who *invented* the whole fucking thing?"

"So let's say they're the good guys," Micky says. "I mean, your Margaret is a founder of the program. All she's ever done is help us, right? So releasing the good guys would be the right thing to do? Right?"

Ava opens her mouth, then shuts it again.

"I say we put it to a vote," Bill says. "And then we learn more about the code and how the stasis capsules work. I mean, it's great if we can open any of them safely and avoid another death like Sloboda's, but there's so much we don't know about the Chipped technology."

Markus nods at his words. "Bill's right. We need to think about this. I mean, who's to know if the Chipped could track us when we open a capsule? What if they can track Sloboda's chip? None of us knows how this technology works."

"No, she was Unchipped," Luna says. "Her chip was never able to integrate with any aspect of the system. They can't track her."

"Yes, but we don't know if these four people are Chipped or not, we don't know why they're in the capsules, and don't know if the capsules themselves are part of the Chip-System," Markus says.

Ava nods. "This is crazy. We don't know shit. I mean, what if turning the capsules off will send some sort of an alarm to Solomon? We'd be as good as dead in a few hours."

"What-if games sound like a poor plan to me," Yeti says. "And guessing is just as useless. I agree with Bill. We should vote."

Kaarina looks up from her hands and investigates the faces around the table. Bill shrugs and starts tapping her. *You're the man, Kay. Do your thing.*

"Shut up, Bill."

Then Kaarina clears her throat and sits taller in her chair. "All in favor of leaving the capsules alone, raise your hands."

Ava and Markus raise their hands.

"All in favor of waking up the founders?"

Yeti and Luna raise their hands without hesitation. Micky looks at Bill, tapping him from across the table. *"We going home or staying, Beau? Now's the time to decide."* Bill shakes his head and dodges Micky's questioning stare. Maria's dark face, her teasing eyes and half-smile flicker through his mind. Even if he did go back to California, even if he somehow found Maria stored away in an underground capsule, he'd need to know how to get her out safely.

Bill raises his hand. Micky and Kaarina follow his lead.

Ava scoffs. "You're all fucking insane." When Yeti reaches out to pat her shoulder, Ava tries to push him away. Bumping into him makes Ava stumble backward. "Get the fuck out of my way, caveman." Yeti raises his hands and steps aside. Ava storms out of the room.

Markus gets up, gesturing for everyone to sit back down. "No, no. It's better if I go after her. We voted the same way. If she agrees to talk to anyone, it'll be me." He walks to the door, stops, and turns to look at the round table.

"I just really, *really* hope you guys know what you're doing."

The pool area is empty; the children are gone. Micky's collecting plastic mugs abandoned here and there around the deck chairs. He's humming something, adding a few Spanish words now and then. Bill recognizes the song but doesn't know its name. They used to listen to it back at the mansion, when devices like computers and pads were still everyday necessities rather than forbidden things to be feared and avoided.

Bill sits by the bar, sipping his fifth margarita. The alcohol has gone to his legs, making them wobbly and tingly. His mind keeps veering from a pink taco stand across the globe to the humming stasis capsules downstairs. The CS-key is upside down in front of him. He has filled in the final supply order, but he hasn't pressed the send button. Two tabs remain open on the computer; the order page and the black market travel auction page. He has enough money to leave. To bring Micky with him. They could leave tonight while everyone is asleep. Nobody would know—not until Micky and Bill are sipping cocktails on a private jet, somewhere high above the Atlantic.

Luna and Kaarina have disappeared into the basement. The two are obsessed with the capsules, the chipping helmets, the memory stick Margaret once gave them. Convinced that Laura Solomon's mother will be able to help them, they've lost themselves in the CS-key programs. Diving into secret files and instructions—all while popping pain pills to keep their Unchipped brains from being hurt by the Chip technology.

Carrying a tall stack of mugs, Micky opens the door that leads back into the hotel. At the same time, Yeti walks out, drying his hair with a white hotel towel.

Micky says something to the man, flashes a smile, and disappears into the hotel. Yeti walks to the bar, opens the fridge, and takes out a bottle without a label. He pushes the cap between his teeth and pops it open.

"That's bad for your teeth, you know," Bill says. He pushes the CS-key forward on the counter and leans his arms against the cool marble surface. "Not many dentists around here if you chip a tooth."

A grunt. That's all he gets from the man. Yeti brings the bottle to his lips and gulps down half the beer. Then he leans against the fridge and stares into space.

"Beautiful night, huh?" Bill says.

"Hmm."

"I think I heard the horses in the barnyard. It's cool how they're coming back."

Another grunt.

"Makes Kaarina real happy."

Yeti's eyes meet Bill's. His expression is blank as he stares. The scars around his face make the man seem older than he is. But in reality, Bill knows he's not much older than Kaarina is. Yeti brings the bottle back to his lips, gulps down what's left. Then he tosses the empty bottle into a metal bin, turns around, and picks out another beer. Teeth clank against the cap before he spits it out and takes a sip.

"You two get along better these days?" Bill asks. He bites his lower lip and looks past Yeti's serious eyes. He shouldn't bring this up. It's none of his business.

"Yes."

"Good, good." *Just drop it*, he thinks. *Leave it alone.* "Because back in the day, it was hard for you two to be in the same room with one another."

Yeti takes another sip, his eyes lingering on Bill.

"It's like she was pancakes," Bill says. "And you ketchup."

Yeti's stare is starting to burn Bill's cheeks.

"Didn't really go well together—"

"What's your point, Yankee?"

Bill moves his finger against the edge of the margarita glass. He shrugs, then grins. "When did it start, then?"

"What?"

"Oh, come on. I saw you at the graveyard. How long have you two been a thing?"

Yeti grunts and shrugs. "Not long." He takes a sip of beer and looks up at the horizon. The moon is out, shining on the concrete basin of the empty pool.

"It was her who started it, wasn't it?" Bill asks. When there's no reply, he continues. "I always knew she liked you, you know. She's just too stubborn to admit it. Micky said it first, back in California. It's just funny how…" Bill stops talking as Yeti reaches for his margarita glass. He tosses the paper umbrella on the ground and empties the drink into his mouth. Bill smiles and sighs for his stolen drink. He reaches for the CS-key but doesn't turn it around.

"I take it that you don't want to talk about it?"

"No."

"Fine, fine. Just making small talk. Should have remembered you Finns are not big fans."

A grunt.

Bill flips the CS-key around. After making sure Yeti can't see the screen, he checks the travel auction tab. No new offers. He's still winning. He flips the screen to face the counter again and looks back at Yeti. "Do you ever get homesick?"

"What?"

"Homesick. Do you ever wish you could go back to Finland?"

Yeti sets down the margarita glass and tosses the empty beer bottle into the metal can. Then he turns around and takes two bottles out of the fridge, pops them open with his teeth. He places one of them next to the CS-key. "Let's say I did," he says. "What difference would it make?"

Bill takes the beer bottle, sniffs it. He's never been a beer drinker, not even back when he had the luxury of choosing between hundreds of brands and styles. He takes a sip anyway. "I think it matters. What you feel. What we all feel."

"Hm."

"I mean, why do the Chipped get to decide what kind of world we live in? Why are they the only ones who get to create cities and products and alternate realities?"

A frown appears on Yeti's face. "Meaning?"

"Meaning, what if we were to do the same? But without them?"

"We are doing it, Bill. That's why you designed the resort and made a plan to become self-sufficient. Live off the land. That's why you ordered the supply."

Bill's eyes flicker to the CS-key. He clears his throat but doesn't say anything.

"You did send the order in, right?"

Bill takes a gulp of beer, buying himself time.

"Bill? Tell me you made the order."

He sets down the bottle and looks up. He forces a smile. "Of course I did. It's just that the shipping takes longer than we thought. That's all."

"How long?"

"Not the usual three days." Bill can't stop himself from blinking rapidly. "More like six or seven days. Maybe longer."

A grunt. Yeti finishes his beer, tosses the bottle, and turns to leave. "Whatever. As long as you sent it in. For a moment there, I thought you were jumping ship." Yeti stops by the counter, standing an inch too close to Bill. "But we both know you wouldn't do that, would you, Bill? Sacrifice hundreds of lives, our new freedom… just because one night, you got a bit weepy and homesick?"

Bill holds his breath. Yeti's right. Of course, he's right.

"*Right*, Bill?"

Bill leans back on his barstool to gain distance from the mountain of a man. "Right. Right! Of course I made the order. Don't be silly. Why the hell wouldn't I?"

Yeti's dark green eyes investigate his face. After a

moment that seems like a small eternity, the man grunts and takes a step back. His footsteps echo in Bill's ears long after he's walked back to his room to wait for Kaarina to return from the basement.

Bill empties his lungs, breathing out his relief. Then he flips the CS-key around and checks the tab.

No new auction offers. He's still winning.

"Morning, sunshine!" Micky greets Bill from the resort's kitchen. Two kids run past him, nearly making Micky drop the wooden tray he's holding. "Hey, watch it!" he yells and then murmurs, "You crazy minions..."

Bill walks over and grabs two pieces of toast from the tray. Then he sits down at the kitchen table. He looks around the cafeteria; most of the kids have already finished their breakfast. Yeti and Markus sit at one of the long tables, quiet, sharing a pot of hot coffee. The Chipped and Unchipped Finns pick up their plates, forming a neat line by the kitchen counter to leave their dishes.

"*Kiitos!*" they yell at Micky, who grins and waves at them happily. "*De nada!*"

"Why don't you just speak English, so everyone can understand?"

"It means you're welcome."

Bill rolls his eyes at Micky. "My Spanish is shitty, but not *that* shitty, Micky."

"And *kiitos* means thank you."

Another eyeroll. "I'm also capable of putting two and two together."

Micky walks over and gently slaps Bill on the back of his head with a kitchen towel. "Bad night? You were talking in your sleep again."

"Yeah? In Spanish or in Finnish?"

Micky laughs and pinches Bill's cheek again. Then he heads straight to the dirty dishes by the kitchen counter and starts collecting them for washing. For him, things haven't changed that much since they lived at the mansion.

"Do you ever wish Maria was here?"

Bill's question surprises himself more than Micky. Plates balanced against his wrist, Micky stops to think. A quick frown shadows his face until he continues to clean up after breakfast. "You know I do, Beau. I'd love to have her here with us. Why do you ask?"

Bill bites into his toast. He shouldn't have brought it up. Not with Micky. His heart might be pure gold, but for him to keep a secret would be like Yeti suddenly enjoying small talk.

"Ava already have breakfast?" Bill asks.

"Nope. Won't come out of her room. Markus left a tray outside her door."

Great. A moping teenager is the last thing they need right now.

"And Kaarina? Luna?"

Micky tosses the towel over his shoulder and closes the industrial dishwasher. The machine starts humming. "Haven't seen them since the meeting."

Could they still be in the basement? Bill shoves the rest of the toast into his mouth and gets up. He walks to the cafeteria side and looks around. "Any coffee left?"

Micky nods at the kitchen counter, where what's left of the breakfast he's served remains. Bill picks out a thermos and three plastic cups. Then he walks to the lobby, sets the coffee down, and tries the basement door. Locked. Yellow light pierces through the gap between the door and the floor. He knocks on the door, clears his throat. "Kay? Open up, Kay."

Nothing happens. They're most likely staying as far as they can from the staircase's yellow light. They're also most likely ignoring him so that they can focus on the task at hand without anyone bombarding them with questions. Bill taps for Kaarina, then Luna. *Hey, quit hoarding the Chipped hellhole. Why do you guys get to have all the fun?* No answer. Bill leans his forehead against the basement door. They're not supposed to go down there. Not until they've learned more about the capsules and the technology that goes with them.

Guys?

Nothing.

I have coffee.

The door clicks and unlocks itself. Bill takes a few deep breaths before stepping into the yellow light.

The tinted glass feels hard against Bill's forehead. He stares at a woman with slick, black hair that twirls around her naked body like a poisonous river. She looks Asian. She also looks angry, even in her unconscious state.

"Wouldn't you be angry? Stuffed inside one of those things?" It's Micky, tapping Bill from upstairs. He's still in the kitchen, slicing tomatoes for a tray full of sourdough bread, lettuce, cucumbers, and canned soy-meat.

Quit spying on me, Micky.

Kaarina walks over and nods at the capsule. "Eerie stuff, right?" She taps the glass with her fingernail. "Her name is Meixiu Tang. She's been in there for over three years."

Bill takes a step back but keeps his gaze on the woman wearing a helmet with wires attached. "Her hair. How come it's not shaved like the rest of them?"

Kaarina shrugs. "The files don't give that kind of information. Luna's only found out their identities, origins, some notes on their work with the program, and the day of capsuling."

Bill nods at the capsule next to Meixiu Tang's. "And this guy?"

"Basile Keller. Used to rule the United Inland." Kaarina walks past Basile Keller, continues to the next capsule. "This here is Timofei Grisin. A former head of the Happiness-Program in City of Russia."

"Who's in charge now?"

"We don't know."

Bill walks to the last of the four stasis capsules. A

seventy-something-year-old woman with short blonde hair rests in it, sleeping peacefully with a tranquil look on her face. "And this is Momma Solomon."

"Not quite." Kaarina joins Bill beside the capsule. "Her name is Marjaana Salonen, but the file describes her as Mrs. Salonen. The owner and founder of Pharma Salonen, later known as Solomon Foundation."

Bill leans in closer to investigate the deep wrinkles on Mrs. Salonen's face. "The company that invented the Happiness-Program."

"That's the one."

"So she started all this?" Bill knocks on the tinted glass. "She's to blame that we're at war?"

They both stare at the woman in silence. Further down the room, Luna sits on a metal counter, her fingers tapping on a glowing purple CS-key. An untouched mug of cold coffee rests next to her on the table. A deep frown on her face, the Serbian woman curses every now and then. Her eyes flicker among the multiple screens spread all around her.

Bill nudges Kaarina gently on the shoulder and nods toward Luna. "Is she okay?"

"She's fine." Kaarina shrugs and crosses her arms on her chest. "I mean, she has a temper for sure. And she can't stand people interrupting her work."

"That's a lot of responsibility for one person. Can't we help her?"

"Not a good idea."

"I mean, I'm no programmer," Bill says, "but I'm

okay with computers. I should at least offer my help—"

Kaarina grabs Bill's arm before he has time to take another step closer to Luna and the metal counter. "Trust me. Interrupt her, and she'll rip you into little pieces."

Bill stops and faces Kaarina. "Jesus on a bike. Was she raised by wolves?"

Kaarina smiles and stares at her friend, completely lost inside a world of malware, coding, and secret files. "I'd say it's the other way around."

Just then, Luna lets out a strange squeal. She sits up on the counter, her hands momentarily frozen above the keyboards and screens. "*Jebote!*" she yells. Then she leans over the purple light, hands tapping even faster than before.

Kaarina and Bill exchange a look.

Did she find something? Bill taps and asks Kaarina.

"*Constantly. She does that.*"

Screams out loud and then continues like nothing happened?

"*Mhm. I've been listening to it all night. It's killing me.*"

They walk over to the metal counter. At the same time, a distant knock on the basement door reaches their ears. Micky's voice appears in Bill's head. "*Open up, amigos. Or I'll feed these sandwiches to the beasts outside.*" Kaarina and Luna look up at Bill and then the door. Micky's tapping them all. Luna refocuses on the CS-key and puts on a set of noise-canceling headphones. It takes Bill a moment to recognize them.

"Hey, are those my—"

"Yes. And just leave it alone, please," Kaarina says and starts walking toward the yellow stairs. Micky's knuckles now rap repeatedly on the door.

"I'm telling you, the beasts are getting close."

"I thought you were against giving the dogs people food," Kaarina says, tapping Micky back.

"I was talking about the kids. Now open up."

While Kaarina heads up to let Micky in, Bill sidesteps to get a look at Luna's screens. The purple light sends sharp pain through his skull. Green numbers and letters flash on the screen. New windows open and close. Luna seems to be in a trance.

Micky's voice gets closer. Kaarina laughs at something he's saying, her mouth full of sandwich. They stop next to the counter. "Hey, Beau! Hi, Lulu!"

Luna doesn't greet Micky back. Bill gestures for him to leave the hacker to her work. "She's busy, Micky. And she hates that nickname, by the way."

Micky sets the tray next to the computers by the counter Luna's sitting on. "Don't shoot the mailman."

"The messenger," Kaarina corrects Micky.

"What?"

They both wave him off at the same time. Micky grabs a sandwich and steps closer to Luna. Tilting his head, his mouth full, he leans closer to see the open laptop next to the glowing purple CS-key. "Whab all thib?" Crumbs land on the keyboard. Luna's hand jerks suddenly, and Micky's snack goes flying.

"What the hell?"

Luna's eyes haven't left the CS-key screen. Then, she freezes again. Bill takes a peek at the screen but can't make sense of what he's seeing.

"What Lu?" he asks. "You found something, didn't you?"

She keeps staring at the screen, a smile slowly spreading across her face. Kaarina puts half of a sandwich back on the tray and reaches for Luna's headphones. Luna dodges Kaarina's hand, keeps her eyes on the screen. Kaarina waves her hands in front of her.

"For the love of dog, would you take off your headset?"

"You mean *my* headset?" Bill says.

"Shut up, Bill."

Luna looks up from the screen, grinning. Finally, she takes off the headphones and hands them to Bill. "Sorry, I borrowed them last time I used your CS-key. Must have put them in my bag and..."

"Never mind the damn gadget," Kaarina says. "What did you find? Do you know how to use the capsules now?"

Luna's smile deepens. "Nope. That's not it."

"Did you figure out if the founders are good guys or bad guys?" Micky asks.

Luna shakes her head. "Not the slightest idea."

"Secret passageway then?"

"Nope."

"Christ on a crutch," Bill says, fingering the headphones nervously. "You clearly figured something out, so spit it out before Micky's head explodes."

Luna sits taller on the counter. Carefully, she flips the CS-key around to get a break from its piercing light. "Well, first of all," she says. "We already suspect that Margaret's memory stick will open the capsules. But looking into her work led me to more information about the Chipped technology in general." Luna reaches for a sandwich and stuffs half of it into her face. Mouth full, she continues, "Secomb...." She stops to take a sip of cold coffee. "Second of all, the Chipped believe they are working for the greater good. That they're the good guys. In their reality, that makes us the bad guys. So, who are we to decide whether the capsule-people are saints or devils?"

Kaarina buries her face in her hands. "Luna, we've been up all night. I'm too tired for riddles. And you already said there's no secret tunnel or whatever Micky here thinks it is you're hiding from us, so for the love of—"

"I found a power switch."

They all stare at her. Luna takes another bite of her sandwich, chews it while the grin on her face gets even madder.

Bill steps closer and sets the headphones down on the counter. "A what now?"

Luna finishes her breakfast, drinks the rest of the

coffee, and wipes her hands clean. "You heard me. A power switch. It's connected with the Chip-System in the city. And not just any city, the headquarters. City of Finland."

Kaarina crosses her arms on her chest. "Luna, can you please just pretend that we're all Owena's age and tell us what it is you found."

"It's basically the city blueprint. The design work, coding, plans… Once I've gone through this all, I can read the city like an open book." She twitches with excitement. "And then… I can reverse it. I guess we can't really know how broad the shutdown is and what it includes. Or how the ones with a functional brain implant will react when it all goes down… But this way, the capsules might not have to be opened manually. Not if I can enter the code into the system. The capsules would still open, and the people inside would get a chance to escape. No need to open each stasis capsule individually with a memory stick. If they can walk, I mean. Hmm.. I'll need to think about this. Because sure, we can get the pods open, but is it safe? And coming out of stasis must be the worst hangover anyone's ever experienced. I mean, unless the capsule heals all of that too…"

"Luna, slow down."

"And of course a lot depends on whether they have a backup set up or not."

"Lu, hold on—"

"Now that I think about it… I don't think they have

a backup. Because this *is* the backup. In case of a catastrophic emergency in the city. Like someone turning off the Chip-System in City of Finland. Or a serious glitch in the system, or, or…"

"Jesus on a—"

"Ha! Yes! I guess they wouldn't see it coming. Interesting. Either way, it'll still take hours of programming to get into their database and the servers, but if the system is down, all their cyber-terror experts will be busy bringing it back up. Maybe we can even destroy the system for good. If I hack into the super-computer that holds the nano—"

"Stop, stop, stop, stop, stop!" Bill raises his hand. "Take a fucking breath, girl. Before I tie your nerdy ass into a knot." He leans against the metal counter and lets his head drop. "You're telling us you can shut down—what—Doctor Solomon's computer?"

Luna reaches for a second sandwich. She picks out two slices of vegan-egg, setting them aside on the table. "Not just that," she says, still investigating what the bread contains. Then she looks up, her burning gaze flickering from one face to another.

"I found a switch to shut down City of Finland."

CHAPTER 3
AVA

The tennis ball hits the ceiling and bounces back into Ava's hand. A steady rumbling sound—her empty stomach—fills the room and makes her twist in discomfort. The food is just outside the door. On a tray, cold for sure, but ready to be eaten. But to give in to her hunger and accept the peace offering would mean that she approved of what the others have decided to do. The shittiest, craziest plan Ava has ever heard.

She tosses the tennis ball again. On its way back down, Ava becomes distracted by a shadow outside her window. The ball hits her in the face.

"Pig-ass-motherffff…" Rubbing her face, she gets up and walks to the window. Annoyed and hungry, she flings the curtains aside. When she sees what stands outside, all trace of anger leaves her body.

"Here horsey-horsey…"

The white horse lifts its head from the bushes. Eyes soft and friendly, it stares at Ava while it continues to munch on dead leaves. Ava climbs onto the writing desk. Slowly, she opens the window and sits down on the sill—only a few feet away from the chomping animal.

"You alone out here, friend?"

The horse snorts and keeps eating.

"Makes two of us. Is your herd somewhere nearby? I bet you have a lot of friends, pretty girl like you." The hooves wander closer to Ava. Soon, the animal is close enough for her to reach out and touch. Ava sits still, hugging her legs against her chest.

"I've got a herd too, I guess," she whispers. "But one that has gone bloody bonkers."

The horse looks up, its long white forelock covering most of its face. Ava can't resist any longer, she reaches her hand to move the rough hair out of the horse's eyes.

"There. Is that better? Don't you guys even groom each other? Take care of each other's coats and that sort of thing? I think I saw it on the telly once. Or was it apes…"

The horse's soft muzzle fumbles Ava's arm, tickling her bare skin. She huffs, scratches the horse on its neck.

"Sucks, huh? Not having someone to take care of you. I mean really look after you." Dirt and sand now cover her fingertips and lodges under her nails, but Ava doesn't care. She keeps scratching. "I mean I have Markus. He's like the big brother I never had. But that's not what I mean. I mean, you know, a guardian. Don't get me wrong, she was crazy. Do you know what that means, White—Can I call you that?"

The horse pulls her head back, pokes Ava in her side, and goes on searching for dead leaves under the window.

"Yeah, White. Enyd was a nutter. But she did take care of us. Like nothing else ever mattered. As long as we were safe, she couldn't care less about anything that was going on in the world. I mean, she would beat us, White. Drug us. Blackmail us to behave. But still… sometimes, I miss…"

The knock on the door startles White. Ava curses under her breath. "Shh, it's okay," she whispers. "If we're real quiet, I bet they'll—"

Another knock. The horse snorts, turns around and takes off toward the fields that begin right outside the yard.

Repeated knocking. "Ava?" Markus's voice.

Who else? This is the second time he's come knocking. The second time she'll ignore him.

"Ava, you need to come soon. They're all in the basement waiting. Kaarina wants you there. We all do."

Ava drops her leg off the windowsill but doesn't jump down. Her anger bubbles back to the surface.

"Oh yeah? Well, tell Kaarina it's not a good time. Besides, why do they need me for anything at this point? We voted already. So bring on the dead dictators. But I'd rather stay locked up here while those who decided to set the world on fire roam around the hotel."

"It's not just the capsules. This is about something

else. They found a switch."

"A what now?"

"Can you please open the door, Ava? You've been in there sulking for—"

"Don't tell me what to do, Markus! You're not my dad!"

"Ava, I'm five years older than you."

Ava jumps down and reaches for the tennis ball on the bed. She throws it—as hard as she can—against the door. "Then stop treating me like I'm fucking five years old!"

For a while, nothing happens. Then Markus's footsteps echo against the corridor walls as he walks away. Ava throws herself on the bed and pushes her face into a pillow. After a muffled scream, she reaches her hand out for the phone. She keeps it turned off—not because Kaarina told her to, but to save the battery. She can borrow the charger, but is always afraid someone will notice it missing. Margaret will text her any day now. Ava knows she's alive, she has to be. She's too important, too smart to be anything but.

Under the pillow, Ava holds the smartphone's power button down for three seconds. She knows she shouldn't have the device with her; it's still connected to the Chip-Net. But if Margaret is kept prisoner somewhere, pumped full of blockers... No, the phone must stay. And it's not like anyone in the city knows she still has it. Only Enyd had known, and she's as dead as operation Kinship Care.

Dim yellow light appears on the screen. She taps the envelope icon.

0 NEW MESSAGES

"Fuck, fuck, fuck..."

Ava hurls the phone against the wall. It bounces off and lands neatly next to her on the second pillow. Margaret's last message is now open on the screen.

SENDER: M.

KEEP THEM SAFE. DON'T FIGHT THEM. I'LL COME FOR YOU.

"Ava? You in there? Open up. We need to talk."

Yeti's voice. Behind her door. She must have fallen asleep after her outburst at Markus. A pink color rises on her cheeks; she shouldn't have lashed out at Markus. Other than Ava herself, he was the only one smart enough to vote for safety. And not to wake up the ancient, blood-lusting maniacs downstairs.

"Ava, we're in this together. All seven of us. Like it or not." Kaarina's voice.

Whatever.

"I found out something really cool, Ava." Luna. "You're going to love this."

She presses the pillow harder against her ears.

"Please, Ava," Markus says. "We're a team."

Behind the door, a bag of some sort rattles with what sounds like an endless supply of tiny glass bottles.

"What's that sound?" Ava can't help but asking.

"I found a motherload of mini bottles of booze in one of the hotel rooms," Micky says.

"What kind of booze? Got anything sweet?"

"I mean, sure. Mint chocolate and blueberry shots, but Ava, you're underage——"

The door flies open. Micky murmurs *gracias* and walks in while Ava returns to sit on the bed.

"What is it? What's so important?"

They all crowd in; Bill, Kaarina, Yeti, Markus, and Luna. Ava pokes something hard on the bed. Before anyone can see the forbidden device, she tucks the smartphone back under the pillow. Bill grabs the tennis ball and sits in the gaming chair. With one leg thrown over the armrest, he bounces the ball against the wall.

Micky walks to the writing desk against the wall, sets out seven plastic cups and a series of tiny plastic bottles of booze. One by one, they all walk over and pick the flavor they like. Feeling Markus's burning gaze at her back, Ava walks over and picks out two mint chocolate shots. Markus is the only one who hasn't visited the stash.

Luna raises her glass to Ava and smiles. "We have something to celebrate. Let's toast."

Ignoring everyone while they open their bottles, raise their glasses to one another, and pour the alcohol down their throats, Markus leans against the door. "Luna's found something," he says. His voice is calm, friendly. There's not a trace of the bitterness or frustration Ava would feel if someone had been a dick to her the way she had been to Markus earlier in the day.

Luna approaches, sits next to Ava on the bed, and produces a blinking purple CS-key. Ava winces but doesn't turn away. Instead, she empties her second bottle of mint chocolate, doing her best to hide the fact that it burns her innards unpleasantly on its way down to her stomach. "While hacking into the Happiness-Program and the founder files to find instructions for the capsules—"

"The death-capsules," Ava corrects Luna.

"Yes… those. While searching for more information and instructions, I got brief access to the supercomputer at the headquarters. The nanotechnology behind the chip—"

"Luna, please." Ava tilts her head. "Spare me the nerd-talk. Just tell me what you found."

"Right. I found a switch."

Ava looks at Luna. Then at everyone else in the room. Most of them are nodding, tossing empty mini bottles into the trash can by the desk. A crooked smile on Yeti's face tells her that whatever this nonsense is, it shouldn't be a bad thing. But then again, this crew— Ava's herd—has proven its madness before.

"Okay, I'll bite. What does this switch do?"

"It turns off City of Finland."

Ava looks at Yeti. His muscled arms crossed on his chest, he grins like the maniac he is.

"Turns off… I don't get it. Like a power outage? I'm sure they have generators and shit over there."

"No, no. Not just electricity. But the AR-reality. The glasses. The capsules. Tiles. All of it."

Ava stares at Yeti and shakes her head. Then she closes her eyes and hears the memory of Margaret's voice in her mind. *Keep them safe.*

"Why would we do that? Is it safe to do that? I don't know... I mean, how does turning off their city really benefit us in any way?"

"Think about all those people they use down in the basement," Kaarina says. Her words have started to slur. She must have already been drinking before the group came here. For some reason it surprises Ava to see Kaarina knock back shots just like everyone else in the room. She must be under a lot of stress, or something. "Ava, what if we could set them free? Help them get their lives back? We could create a whole new city of our own, with no mind control, or pills, or brainwashing. Something real and safe. If we got those people out, there's no way the city could put them all down at once. There are thousands of people plugged into their CS server. Maybe millions."

"And where are they supposed to go once they wake up naked and alone? Hop out of their prison and fly... where? Here?"

"If they'd like. Yes."

"And how are you going to bring them over?" Ava bites her lower lip in frustration. "I mean it's a nice thought and all. But you're risking all of us for just that. For a nice thought. What if they'll see who pulled the switch? What if they can see where we are?"

"Obviously we'll need to make sure—"

"Nothing seems to be obvious to you! You haven't thought this through at all. How do we even know that shutting off the server will open the capsules? It could just power them down and end the life support for the people in there. No, we need to wait for Margaret. She will know what to do. Any moment now, she'll contact me—"

"We can't put all our eggs in Margaret's basket," Kaarina says, shaking her head. "I know the plan is not perfect..." Ava gives her a dirty look. "At least not yet it isn't. There's a lot more research to be done, of course. But we can build on this. We've got skills. Talent. I mean, look at what Luna's figured out, all by herself! She's studying the programming of the world's most powerful system. The more files we access and research, the more we understand. And the more we understand, the better we will be able to take down the sick world Solomon has created."

Yeti huffs. "Besides... We're telling you that we've found a way to take down the most powerful city in the world and release all the people there the Chipped have ever captured... and you're telling us it's not *worth* it?"

Markus's hands wave in the air, gesturing for a truce. "Okay, okay. Ava has a point. What if it's not safe? It's great that Luna has all this information. And sure, let's dig some more. Why not? But it took them years to build the city. Hundreds or thousands of programmers to build the

CS. To learn only a fraction of this technology will take time. A lot of time. And we still might not understand it all. I'd love to close down the city and get those capsules open as much as you would. That would be a fair payback for everything they've done to you…" Markus clears his throat. "I mean to us…"

Yeti cocks his head. "Oh, is that what you're saying? You don't think this concerns you, do you? Chip-Head?"

"Of course it concerns me. Just because I'm properly Chipped—"

"Oh, and we're not *proper*?"

Markus closes his eyes, clearly counting to ten. It must be hard to be the only sober person in the room. Kaarina steps between him and Yeti. "We don't use those… *titles* here. And need I remind you, Markus is not the only Chipped here. Plenty of people with Chips in their brains, some worked back in the city, some didn't. And we've all found a way to co-exist. So what difference does it make now? Solomon used us all as pawns equally while she played God."

"Of course you would take his side," Yeti says and nods at Markus. "Ever since the beginning, you've chosen him. No matter what he says."

A short laugh escapes Markus's lips. He stares at Yeti, then at Kaarina, then back at Yeti in disbelief. "She chose *me*? How drunk are you, exactly?" He huffs a bit, tucks his chin. Kaarina and Yeti exchange a nervous look.

Luna throws another empty bottle into the trash can. The CS-key rests screen-down on the bed. "So... anyway," she says. "It's a no-go then? The kill switch?"

"That's not what I said," Markus huffs out. "Just that we shouldn't rush into anything."

"And we won't." Kaarina gives him a half-smile. "We'll be careful. But timing is everything. We do need to act before Solomon finds out we have all this information."

Bill shrugs and palms the ball. Several empty bottles lie on his lap, but he seems oblivious to them. He spins the gaming chair so he can face the rest of them. "I hate to be a party pooper... but you *do* understand it would mean war? It'd be like us releasing their war prisoners."

"What else is new?" Kaarina asks. "We've been at war with them ever since we fled. And Luna says they can't track us. This is just a way to get back at them, lots of pros with no cons. Attacking her city would leave Solomon vulnerable. Those who wanted to leave the city could do so. There's no way they have enough guards to hold thousands of people. They'd all get a fresh start."

A ringing sound in her ears, Ava closes her fists around the bedsheet. "You're insane! What if they all die like Sloboda did?"

"Ava, Sloboda was so sick that the only thing keeping her alive was the capsule."

"You don't know that! And who cares what happened, she's dead! You know shit! And what do you mean, there are no cons? Even if the pods open, all those people will wake up in a dark pod somewhere, naked and terrified. Nothing about this is safe!" The anger is becoming too much to bear. Missing her mother, missing Margaret… it's slowly driving Ava mad. And now, these fools want to mess with the only thing that's good in her life: Iceland. Her safe haven.

"She *must* pay for what she's done!" Everyone in the room turns to stare at Kaarina. "She must!" It's the first time ever they've witnessed her raising her voice like this. Drunk or not, it's unnerving to see her this way.

"Hey…" Bill has recovered from his surprise first. "We all want the same thing here, Kay. We'll figure this out. Just chill. Have another drink."

"Yeah, because that'll solve it all," Ava huffs, but takes a sip from her cup, eying the pillow on the bed. They would change their drunken minds if she told them about Margaret's text message. But then they'd also take the phone from her. What if Margaret needs their help and can't tap her? How is she supposed to connect with them if the phone is shut off?

Margaret told them to wait. To not fight against the Chipped. And now these crazy people are digging into files, hacking super computers, rushing to conclusions… Doing exactly what Margaret told them *not* to do.

Before she can think, Ava reaches for the CS-key and snatches it from Luna. She throws the computer across the room. It hits the bathroom door hard, then clatters to the floor. Eyes wide, Luna stares at the device on the floor. "*Ti si jebeni kreten!*"

Bill freezes on the gaming chair. "Whatever she said, I don't think it was a compliment, Ava, but I agree with Luna. What the fuck?"

Luna glares at Ava. Her eyes are filled with rage. If Ava didn't know her better, she'd be scared Luna would punch her on the nose. Shit. She shouldn't have done that.

Luna storms over and scoops up the CS-key from the floor. "I had the connection open! You could have killed everything I've—"

The CS-key starts vibrating. A purple light appears, and the screen seems to come to pieces in front of them. Luna holds the computer, looking up as the hologram appears and fills the center of the room.

"Shit, shit, shit…" Luna taps frantically at the computer, but the hologram keeps getting clearer.

Bill looks at the half empty bottle in his hand, reading the label. "What the hell is in this shit?"

Kaarina walks over and holds up her hand. "Hold on… I know who this is."

The hologram-woman looks up, listening to them. She's clearly trying to figure out who she's connected with. Ava sits back on the bed and hugs her legs against her chest, rocking her body back and forth.

Luna sets the computer down on the floor. Kaarina circles the hologram. The image sways slightly, still not saying a word. She presses her index finger to her lips, gesturing for the others to stay quiet. Yeti and Markus join her, all staring at the pale woman with her pointy nose and high forehead.

Luna nods at the computer, staring at Kaarina with eyes wide. Kaarina gestures for her to wait. They all gape at the woman in the hologram. Then the woman speaks.

"Iris? Is that you? I don't have time for your prank calls."

Ava looks at the hologram woman, then at her friends. Yeti and Kaarina glare at the woman, frowning deeply. They clearly know who this is.

"Jovan? Is it you then?"

Luna gasps for air. "Who are you? And what have you done with Jovan?"

The whole room stares at Luna in shock. The alcohol makes the room spin around her, but Ava stands anyway and joins Luna. "Yeah, and while we're at it… Where's Margaret Wilson?"

The hologram-woman stares into space for a few seconds. Then she scoffs. A slight smile appears on her face. "Look at that. Kaarina's crew, finally coming out to play." Kaarina's hands clench into fists, her knuckles whitening. Seeing this woman seems to have sobered her right up. "See, I told Laura you'd be stupid enough to get caught eventually. But never in a million years did I think you'd be stupid enough to call us. Do you even know how easy it is to trace this call?"

Yeti's places his hand on Kaarina's shoulder to stop her from stepping forward and kicking the computer.

Markus circles around, his soft and friendly eyes investigating the hologram. "And how are you this evening, Nurse Saarinen?"

Her head cocks. "Mister Nyman. Is that you?"

"Sure is."

"Had a change of heart then?"

Markus eyes her, calmly circling the hologram. "What's that?"

"Well, it's obvious. You want to come home."

Kaarina scoffs and steps away from Yeti. "And why the fuck would he want to do that?"

Nurse Saarinen half-smiles, raising her eyebrows. "Poor Markus. The only one with a functioning chip in your brain. The only one fully capable of great things. And you still let that scavenger talk for you."

This time Yeti has to wrap his arms around Kaarina to stop her from attacking the woman—even though she isn't really in the room.

"Kaarina's not a scavenger. None of us are. And with all due respect, I'm not the only Chipped who decided to leave the program. The city was a bad place for many of us."

A static silence fills the room as they wait for Nurse Saarinen to reply. Finally, she nods and reaches for something next to her. Soon, a set of AR-glasses appears on her face.

"So that's it then? You just wanted to call me and wag your finger at me? How adorable. And also—a total waste of my precious time."

They all look at each other. Kaarina spreads her hands. Ava leans in to whisper into Luna's ear. "Can they really track us, like she says?"

With wide eyes, Luna stares back at her and shakes her head for a *no*. "They can see that the device belongs to City of Serbia," Luna whispers back. "But that's it."

"Ask her about the capsules."

"Are you crazy?"

Bill steps closer to the hologram, Micky right behind him. "Now that we have you here, Good Nurse… Why don't you entertain us by telling us why you've stuffed people into small tubes underground? I mean, I get that these are hard times and all. But I'm sure you have enough space for everyone. Everyone you haven't gunned down or poisoned to death since The Great Affliction."

Nurse Saarinen takes off the AR-glasses. "Why would I waste my breath explaining anything to you fools?"

Micky shrugs and says, "*No se*. Why the hell not?"

"Make us understand," Markus adds. "Change our minds about the city. If the Happiness-Program is really for our own good, why were so many people unhappy living in your alternate reality?"

With a disinterested look on her face, Nurse Saarinen takes a deep breath. For the longest time, Ava's sure she will break the connection without answering Markus' question. But then her slightly nasal voice fills the room again.

"Convenience," she says. "Humanity's thirst for it has never changed, not even during The Great Affliction. When you think about it, not much has changed since the time before the cities. Smartphones and video games. Social media and alternate realities. Never leaving the house, total isolation, and no real human contact. People couldn't see each other as real beings anymore. It was too easy to tell someone off, fire them, even threaten them when it all took place online."

Ava sits down on the bed. Her eyes flicker to the pillow. She's forgotten to turn the smartphone off.

"There's nothing simpler than the human mind. I can put it in three words for you. One, incivility. Two, insecurity. Three, isolation. People have always been afraid of those who they don't understand. So, what does technology do? It gives these fearful monkeys unlimited access to see and say anything, to misunderstand everything. It wasn't too long until the apes felt as if they could *do* anything as well. And what is the most reactive animal of them all? Spoiler alert, it isn't the dog."

"I'm either more shit-faced than I thought I was," Bill says, "Or you're just pulling words out of your ass. What does any of this have to do with the capsules?"

"Why is everyone always so endlessly fascinated with the stasis capsules? It's just mediocre science. Nothing that we haven't known or been able to do for decades. How about the rest of it? Hm? Why won't you ask about the science that put an end to humanity driving itself to extinction? Ask about the chip that can restore sight to a blind man and give a deaf woman her hearing back. What about the fact that there is hardly any mental illness left in the AR-cities? People lack for nothing. They have companions, homes, jobs, entertainment, fulfillment. They have absolutely all they need, and then some. Nobody's homeless, or starving, lacking clothes. I mean, people even get to have risk-free sex whenever they desire. So no loneliness, either."

"Yeah, sex with a bunch of fucking pixels," Yeti says. "It's just an illusion. None of it is real."

"Have it your way. More STD's and unwanted pregnancies for you. Go for it. It's not surprising, really. All those years, living in the woods like rabid skunks. Humping and killing whatever you could get your hands on."

"Fuck you, you piece of shit."

Nurse Saarinen shrugs and puts on her AR-glasses. "Perfect example of a vocabulary that only a feral animal would use. Now if you'll excuse me. We can pick up this enlightening conversation once Doctor Solomon's men pick you up and put you in time out."

Nurse Saarinen is about to turn off the call. Ava can tell. "Wait!" Ava ignores the pleading looks around her. "We know how to ruin you. And you can't track this call."

"Oh, how cute. Your little hacker friend helped you. Invincible, yeah? That's what you believe?"

"We used Margaret's code—"

Yeti's enormous palm covers Ava's mouth. He's

moved from Kaarina's side to sit with Ava on the bed. Kaarina paces back and forth next to the hologram.

"Maybe we're not invincible, no," Kaarina says. "But we do know a thing or two."

Nurse Saarinen moves the glasses up on her forehead. "Oh, this should be good. What is it you know, Kaarina? Hmm? Other than shoveling shit and running away from smart decisions?"

Ava studies Kaarina, seeing her rage and her need for revenge. No one says a word out loud, but the Unchipped voices echo in Ava's head as they tap for Kaarina and everyone else in the room.

"No. Don't do it."

"Cállate, Kaarina."

"Don't tell this bitch shit. You're drunk and she's provoking you, Kay, it's a—"

"I know how to turn off your city. All of it. I know how to destroy the Happiness-Program. Tell Doctor Solomon that I'm coming for her."

The room falls silent after Kaarina's words. Everyone holds their breath, waiting for Nurse Saarinen's reaction. For a moment, she stares into space, blinking. Then high-pitched laughter pierces the silence. She shakes her head and tucks the AR-glasses back on.

"A bunch of rabid dogs," she says. "That's what you are. A frantic pack of pathetic animals that has no idea what it's doing."

The purple light dims to gray as the hologram disappears.

CHAPTER 4
LUNA

Argument. Hostile words. Bill pulling his hair. Ava screaming for everyone to get the fuck out of her room. It all echoes in Luna's mind, over and over, like a bad scene from one of the Serbian soap operas her mother used to watch on Sunday mornings. The CS-key shoved under her arm, she storms out of the room and runs down the corridor, all the way to the yellow staircase.

The pills rattle in the bottle she's holding. Sitting on the metal counter in the dead-silent basement, Luna tosses two painkillers into her mouth. She flips the CS-key around and fires it up.

Whatever program or access key Ava triggered when she threw the computer against the wall, it's missing now and Luna can't find it. Not even in the recently accessed files and apps.

"How did you do that..." she murmurs and jumps off the counter. Her hiking shoes tap against the yellow tiles as she starts toward the end of the room.

The basement doesn't give her the creeps the way it does Bill and Markus. Even Kaarina seems uncomfortable here. They find the dim light and the low hum of the capsules unnerving. But not Luna. There's something soothing about being surrounded by machines. They're very unlike humans: controllable, easy to understand. Each result was initiated by a command. Each command has a consequence. There's no guessing, no wild cards. The code works according to rules that can't be changed.

She stops by the four occupied stasis capsules. Placing her shoe on the concrete base of the old woman's capsule, Luna jumps up to get to an eye-level look at Mrs. Salonen: Doctor Solomon's mother. Switched off. Forgotten. But why?

Luna feels as if she knows this woman. Reading her history, her logs on the Happiness-Program when it was only an idea in a white paper on her pharmaceutical company's website, gives Luna the impression that this woman was a visionary. A leader. But—unlike her daughter—a humanitarian.

A tranquil face with deep lines encircling closed eyes.

Fine, almost baby-like hair under the chipping helmet.

Pale, hairless arms and a chest covered with dozens of moles.

"Why did she leave you here?" Luna whispers. "What did you do?"

She steps down from the capsule base and reaches

118

for the object hidden in her hoodie pocket. Not once has she turned the device on. No matter how lonely her nights. No matter how desperately she wants to be seen again, to be more than the digital mastermind behind their fight against the Chipped.

The AR glasses seem to melt into her face. They feel as though they're made of silk, not plastic.

"Now what?"

The soldier never gave Luna instructions on how to use these things. There had been no time. What a mindfuck, the whole concept of time. In the farmhouse, tucked away from City of Serbia, she used to have nothing but. Time. Leisure. Reading. Rescuing dogs. Then, she had met him. Another person, so perfectly imperfect, flawed like Luna. And just like that—boom. Time ran out. She had to leave the city, the country, everything familiar and safe. She had to leave him, too.

Luna stares at the capsule's silhouette through the dim lens of the AR-glasses. She stands up taller, lifts her chin.

"Call Jovan."

Three white dots appear in front of her eyes. A soft, robotic voice echoes in her ears.

CALL INITIATED. JOVAN. CITY OF SERBIA.

Luna circles the capsules, running her hand over one tinted glass door after another. She can see Jovan and everything around him. The purple tiles outside the window. The familiar Chip-Center office space, its screens and gadgets. The way the AR-glasses twist Luna's senses and her reality fascinates her. It's like living inside a computer. After she had assured Jovan that she's okay, and that her random call to him was exactly that—random—they've chitchatted about everything but the war that's going on and the Unchipped's existence that is in danger to collapse under its crushing weight.

"I feel like I'm in a video game."

"A video game?" he says. "Not a fast-burn murder mystery? Who are you, and what have you done with Luna?"

She can't help but laugh. "This is too corny to be a book," she says. "No, this is a task. Earn three extra lives by crashing at least a hundred capsules. This is World of War-tubes."

Jovan's soft chuckle sends warm waves through Luna's body. She had forgotten just how much she enjoys his company. His sense of humor. The way he's not afraid to make fun of himself—or of Luna either.

"And Tiny. How is my good girl? I hope you're not letting Wacko bully her."

Just when she thought she couldn't like the man more, he asks about her dogs.

"Ah, I see. You fell for it."

"Fell for what?"

"Tiny's little act of innocence. Trust me, my friend. She's nothing of the sort."

"No?"

"M-mm. She can be the devil himself, if she feels like it. Mischievous as fuck."

Jovan fake-gasps at the end of the line. "You take that back. How dare you talk about my queen like that?"

"Your queen, huh? Tell me now, what kind of a queen licks her own behind and then runs around giving kisses to whoever tries to escape the slowest?"

Another gasp. "I'm warning you. Spreading this false information is a violation of the royal privacy policy. I'm sorry to say, but I need to report you to the authorities immediately."

Luna's smile fades. She lifts the glasses an inch and stares at the rows of capsules in front of her. Prison cells. Four lives, their dignity and freedom of will wiped away.

"Luna? You still there?"

Breath wheezing, she pats her pockets for the inhaler. She's left it by the metal counter she uses as her office. After fast-walking over, she takes a puff and holds the medicine in her lungs.

"Shit," Jovan says. "That was a stupid comment. About authorities and reporting. I got lost in our Queen Tiny story. I'm sorry."

Luna stares at the stack of unused CS-keys on the shelves, counts them from bottom to top. She exhales, then feels the air flowing into her lungs again.

"I shouldn't have brought it up," Jovan continues. "It's never a good topic between us."

"Why?" she asks. "Because you're Chipped and I'm

Unchipped? I thought you of all people would be above labeling others like that."

Jovan's lips press into a thin line as he considers his words. Luna stares at his face, investigating, wondering if she could have misjudged the man. Maybe he's not on her side.

"Those labels. Like it or not, they're a matter of life and death now. We live in a world where our whole future is based on whether or not we have a functioning chip installed."

"So, you're what? Better than me?"

"Your words, not mine. No, Luna. We all play our own part in this. I became a Chipped soldier to save my own life. Now I've become the Facilities Manager. I have access everywhere around the city."

"Whoop-de-doo. Congrats, Chief."

"No. You don't understand. I'm doing this for a reason. Not to keep me alive, but to protect those who are still out there. Including you. What the Solomon Foundation is doing might be terrible, but us going around improvising is a grave mistake."

He might as well have slapped her in the face. Sloboda. The capsule. Had Luna's need to save her ended in her death? Were they all just flying blind?

"Lu? What is it?"

She clears her throat, unsure if she really wants to hear the answer. "Back home... That day when we escaped..." Her voice cracks and she's forced to pause.

"Right. I was there. I remember. Go on."

"We took Sloboda out of stasis. I mean… I took her out."

"Okay. I see where you're going with this."

"I know the capsules have healing capabilities. I know she was as good as dead when she went in."

"You didn't kill her, Luna."

"But I did, though." Her throat is so swollen that it takes her a long time to reply. She appreciates Jovan's patience, waiting silently as she composes herself. "She's dead, Jovan."

He takes a deep breath. "Okay, yes. Your friend is dead. Yes, you took her out of a very complicated piece of technology, and in a completely inefficient and unsafe way. You need a code to open the capsules safely, and only the Happiness-Program founders have those."

Luna swallows loudly. So it is true. Should she tell Jovan she has a memory stick with one of these codes in her possession?

"So yeah. You acted recklessly. That was a mistake. But Lu, Sloboda was long gone when she was put in that capsule. The stasis kept her alive, and the capsule does have healing capacity. But only to a certain point. Her only purpose in the state she was in was to serve the city as processing power—"

"Wait. You're saying that Sloboda was used to power up the AR-city?"

"Of course she was. Everyone in the stasis capsules is. Just like the people who work in the server centers, but permanently. And therefore, in a way—and this is the way I personally look at it—you did the only humane thing there was left to do."

"But I didn't know what I was doing."

"Nevertheless. She's at peace now."

This she can see. She feels it in her chest, her stomach. Jovan's right. And he's telling her the truth. It still makes her angry. Flustered. She changes the subject abruptly.

"I just don't see why you didn't come with us."

"You wouldn't. You're too stubborn to see the bigger picture. Some wars are lost even before they really begin. This is one of them. The Chipped are too powerful."

"So… It is what it is? Is that what you're saying?" Luna huffs. "Give me a break."

"No, that's not what I'm saying." Jovan stops again, hesitating. "Luna, I will tell you everything. When the time is right. But I can't do it now, not like this."

"Like what? Over a piece of stolen CS-technology?"

"Exactly. Saying certain words could trigger the spyware."

Luna reaches for the glasses in horror. "You said the line was safe. If it's not, we need to end this call—"

"No, no. The line is secure. But there is some malware that only Iris has access to. And after they found out about the mole, they've set highly technical words as triggers, words that a programmer would use. So I just need to be sure. To keep you safe."

"Okay, so we need to meet face to face. Is that it? You coming over for a pot of coffee? Should I turn the stove on?"

Silence. His breathing gets heavier. "It would make sense for you to come back home, Bloody Mary. You can do more if you're *in* the system, not running away from it. *That's* what I'm saying."

"Don't call me that. You know I hate that nickname."

"No can do. Suits you too well."

They fall silent, both smiling but dodging each other's eyes. Could she go home? Be part of Jovan's life again? His reality? Iris had told her she was worthy. That she'd have a job as the city's programmer whenever she chose to take it. *Just say the word,* Iris had said. *And your chip will be fixed.* But that was before she'd saved the group of rebels she'd been hired to find, stolen Sloboda from a stasis capsule, and emptied the Chip-Charity accounts of their CC's.

"They know how to do that now? Fix the brain implant? Anyway, Iris would have me arrested."

"No, we need your skills. They're pretty damn close to fixing the malfunctioning chips, from what I've been told."

"Can I think about it?"

Jovan smiles, his soft eyes now looking straight at Luna's as he nods to confirm.

Luna sighs and flips over her CS-key. The purple light is like a tiny dagger stabbing into her skull.

"You still have that old thing?"

"Sure do. I'm working on—"

Jovan's hands wave wildly, gesturing for Luna to stop explaining.

"Ahh," she says. "Right. Trigger words. Gotcha."

"Better safe than sorry."

Luna looks over her shoulder toward the end of the capsule row, where Mrs. Salonen rests peacefully. The old woman would know all the answers. She created the damn things, the whole shebang. Not only would she know about the capsules, but she'd know about the chipping helmets, the CS-system, and every single detail of the nanotechnology behind it all.

The Chipped world. So far away, yet always so near. And now, the person who invented this new world rests in the basement of a hotel in an old city that used to be called Reykjavik.

"I do have a question, though."

Jovan smiles, raising one of his eyebrows. "Use small words. Nothing nerdy."

Luna rolls her eyes but can't fight the smile. Her elbow moves to nudge Jovan, making her almost lose her balance and fall off the counter. The glasses are making her forget which world is which.

"Say I have a distant friend—let's say a colleague— who likes to nap. Like, a lot. All day, every day, she snoozes away in a comfy bed where no-one can interrupt her peace."

"Doesn't sound like a thriller to me," Jovan says.

"It's not. This one's more like a fairytale. Think of *Babaroga*, the chicken-legged old woman who eats people. My sleeping friend is trying to escape from her."

"Gotcha."

"So, one day, my friend goes to sleep but doesn't wake up again. She sleeps one day, then another. Soon, it's been weeks, months, and then years that she's rested in her bed. I start to get worried. So I read books to her, all night, every night. I learn about old folk tales, about witches and wizards, black magic, and spells."

Jovan sucks his lower lip in, focusing on Luna's words, nodding every now and then.

"Finally, I get too tired of waiting. I want my friend to wake up now. I decide to cast a spell to wake her up. The thing is... I really don't know much about my colleague. Her desires, values, and motivations. I know how to proceed, but I'm not sure what is to come."

"I see..."

"So, my question is this. Should I wake up my sleeping friend?"

"I would need to know more about this friend," Jovan says slowly. "But in my experience, playing with this kind of magic is always a risk. You may think you're only trying to do the right thing by helping a friend out, but who's to know what else her awakening will lead to? Sometimes a seemingly small deed can spread and have unintended or unseen consequences."

Luna thinks of the kill switch. Their sweet revenge against Doctor Solomon and those who condemned Luna's kind to be exiled from normal life. The people who decided that those with a malfunctioning chip were yesterday's news, no better than dog food.

"What if it were the other way around?"

Jovan's frown deepens.

"What if I had a magic button? And with this button, I could seek out all the evil witches and turn them into frogs and white rabbits."

Jovan shakes his head slowly. "Luna, no. No, no, no."

"What if I can beat *Babaroga*?"

They sit around the four humming capsules, all staring at Mrs. Salonen's silhouette behind the tinted glass. The smell of fresh grounds fills the air, as they silently sip their morning coffee from yellow plastic mugs. A tray filled with Micky's tuna sandwiches, along with a dozen unsliced sour pickles and a kitchen knife, sits in the middle of their semi-circle, untouched. Just the thought of eating something is too unnerving right now. Eating tuna and pickles for breakfast even more so.

Bill tosses the tennis ball into the darkness. Three dogs surge after it, Ässä barking continuously while Wacko and Tiny focus on hunting for the ball in the dark. Random yellow tiles light up under their paws as they chase each other around the vast underground area. Hearing the dogs play in the basement seems to ease everyone's mind, at least a little bit. Their sheer joy creates a false feeling of normality. As if they weren't gathered here to shut down the most powerful city in the world.

"Are you sure it'll only shut down City of Finland?"

Yeti asks Luna. "What if it's all the cities?"

This gets Bill's attention. "Holy pedaling Jesus! Can we turn off City of California as well?"

Luna raises her hand, telling Bill to calm down. "I'm sure. It's just City of Finland. To turn them all off, I'd need to access each city's main server."

"And can you do that?" Kaarina asks.

"I can. I could. But I would need more time. And didn't we agree that with Nurse Saarinen trying to track us down, we need to act now?"

They all nod.

"Good. As soon as the city is down, they'll need all their resources to bring the system back up. With the intel and experts Laura Solomon has working for her, I'm sure they'll be able to turn the city back on, but I'm not sure how long it'll take them—"

Yeti nods. "But it should be long enough for the capsuled people to get away. And with the founders' code integrated with the kill switch, the capsules will pop open safely?"

"Exactly."

"And you trust Jovan's intel? That the founders' code will open the pods safely?"

It's Luna's turn to nod. "I do. And it makes total sense. Why else would the capsules have a slot for the memory sticks?"

The dogs bring back the tennis ball, dropping it in front of Bill's bare feet. Since the cruise ship, all the dogs have become obsessed with the black man with dreadlocks. Most of Luna's rescues roam around the village now, going around from house to house, begging for extra meals and scratches, only visiting Luna at the hotel. Or more accurately, they visit Micky—at the kitchen whenever he prepares breakfast, lunch, or dinner. The rest of the time they're glued to Bill's side or playing with the children. At nighttime, the dogs like to stay with the kids and the rebel refugees who take care of them. The small cottages aren't much, but so far, no one has complained. People—the Unchipped as well as the Chipped—seem content and grateful for the safe-haven they've found in Iceland.

Wacko nudges Bill's arm, then tucks himself underneath. Bill hugs him back, kissing the yellow mutt's head. Luna smiles; she doesn't mind. It warms her heart to see Wacko getting attached to another human rather than just her. The mutt's ability to judge a person's character is uncanny. And the dog never shies away from anyone who lives at the resort. Not once has he growled or barked at anyone—except for Ava's mother Niina, but that must have been because the Chipped woman didn't let the dog play with Sanna and Owena. After all, Wacko's still just a dog. Play and food rule his world.

But above all, he's among good people now. A great pack—no matter what Nurse Saarinen thinks or says.

Ava raises a hand. She sits next to Markus, leaning on one of the empty capsules. She's been quiet ever since yesterday's incident with the CS-key and Nurse

Saarinen's surprise visit. "I know I don't really deserve a say in this… after yesterday."

Kaarina shakes her head. "You know you do, Ava. Don't be silly."

Ava scratches her head, a nervous habit she has. The chipping scar at the back of her skull tends to bleed and get infected as a result. Luna has never asked her about it. None of them have. Being able to enter each other's minds seems like enough of a privacy violation. They hardly ever ask questions about each other's pasts, their lives before this group came together. In a way, none of that really matters anymore.

"I just thought… I think…"

Markus wraps his arm around the girl, sighing deeply. "She's concerned about safety. And so am I."

"Whose safety?" Micky asks. "Ours or theirs?"

"Both," Ava says, her eyes watering and lips pouting slightly. "My mom… she must know something's going on. She's been locked up with the girls for days. Won't open the door. Won't talk to anyone. It's not just about the Chipped finding us. People are starting to get suspicious. About us and what's going on in the hotel. I think everyone should get a say. We should give them all a vote."

Markus squeezes her and leans his head on the top of Ava's head. "Ava's right. I mean, don't get me wrong." He nods at Luna. "If Luna says they can't trace us, I believe her. But after our chat with Nurse Saarinen, I'm pretty sure it's just a matter of time before they find us."

"And Margaret…" Ava says, her voice cracking as she sobs. "She hasn't messaged me since we left City of Serbia. And she promised… What if she…" Ava's sobs get the best of her, making it impossible for her to speak.

"What if Margaret is captured in the city? What if they avenge our pulling the switch by hurting her?" Markus ends Ava's sentence.

The room falls silent again. Luna sips the last drops of her coffee, wondering if a sandwich would settle her growling stomach. She stares at Ava, considering her worries. Of course the girl has a right to be concerned about Margaret. After all, she loves her. More than anyone, Luna thinks. The deaf woman saved Ava and kept her safe at the Kinship Care children's home when things turned bad. Ava not hearing from her is alarming, to say the least.

Of course Ava would want to know Margaret's not plugged into a capsule somewhere. And until she hears a word from—

Luna's head snaps up when she remembers the missing device. "Ava, what do you mean Margaret hasn't *messaged* you? You mean tapped you, right?"

The girl stops crying and freezes against Markus's chest. Her eyes flicker nervously to Luna and then back to the floor. "Right. I mean, maybe they fixed her chip, so she wouldn't be able to… or maybe she's blocked… I mean, it doesn't matter. Either way, we should wait for her return before we pull some mystery switch that does who knows what."

"No, no. You specifically said she hasn't messaged you. Though she promised, what? To call you? Text? How would you hear from her, when the only devices that are allowed here are the two CS-keys and the computer Margaret gave us?"

Ava twists her hand and buries her face in Markus's shirt. He looks up at Luna with pleading eyes. *"Luna, please. Let her be,"* his eyes seems to beg her. *"She's suffering enough as it is."*

Luna opens her mouth, but no words come out. She can't be too angry at Ava. She also has a secret device. The AR-glasses Jovan gave her. Until yesterday, she would have had a way to defend herself; she'd never used them. But now she has.

Yeti gets up, grunting and staring at Markus and Ava. "Her fucking smartphone. The kid still has it on her."

Markus gets up and stands in front of Ava. His head barely reaches Yeti's chest, but the man stands tall against the mountain that rises in front of him. "You leave her alone. We have all broken the rules here. All of us."

"Oh yeah? You don't see anything blinking or vibrating in my pockets. Step up, Ava. If you got nothing to hide, you won't mind us patting you down, will you?"

Ava stands up but hides behind Markus's back. She's started to sob again. Kaarina stands and walks over, planting herself directly in front of Yeti. Yeti doesn't move an inch.

"Go easy on her," Kaarina says, looking hard into Yeti's eyes. "No one is patting down anybody. This is not that kind of place. We're family. Not enemies."

Yeti scoffs and crosses his arms on his chest. Finally, he steps away from Markus, breaking Kaarina's gaze to stare at Ava's swollen eyes. "This is bullshit. What Chip-Head here said. I haven't broken any fucking rules."

With sad eyes, Markus looks at Kaarina. "It's not about rules. It's about doing things that hurt other people because we want something for ourselves."

Kaarina stands next to Luna, now holding her breath. She's suddenly speechless. Yeti looks at them, then back at Markus. Gritting his teeth, he spreads his hands in defeat. "Fuck it. Who cares. If the kid has a phone, it's just a matter of time before Nurse Saarinen or Solomon or some other Chipped asshole tracks us down. I say we pull the switch. And we pull it *now*."

With one hand, Luna fingers the AR-glasses in her hoodie pocket, her other hand holding the purple CS-key—ready to go. She just needs to trust what she's learned, trust the math and her newly-found knowledge of the Chipped technology, and City of Finland will collapse.

Kaarina sighs, her chin still lowered. Since Luna met the woman, she's never seen her this tired, this defeated. Out of the seven of them, Kaarina has always seemed the least vengeful. But ever since they arrived in Iceland, her behavior has become more and more aggressive. Some days, her talk about Doctor Solomon has bordered on obsession. But now, when the opportunity is only one click away, she seems hesitant again.

With all their voices rising, the basement suddenly sounds like a battlefield. As Bill, Micky, Markus, and Yeti argue, Luna taps for Kaarina. *You okay there, friend?*

Kaarina, standing right beside Luna, doesn't look at her. But her lip twitches. A sad smile spreads on her face.

"I forgot about her. Margaret. Her safety."

Luna doesn't know what to say.

"Every night, ever since we stepped off the boat, I've dreamt of this moment. Getting back at Solomon. Crushing her. Leaving her weak and defeated, picking up the pieces. And all this time, I've had an ally out there—a friend— whose safety didn't even cross my mind."

Luna lets go of the AR-glasses, now holding onto the CS-key with two hands. *You're doing the best you can in a situation where no one knows the right thing to do. You may risk our friend's life. Maybe you won't. But if we open those capsules, we might be saving thousands of lives. Maybe millions. Sure, we can't go over and scoop them all up, but there's no way the city can hide their capsule scheme after this. Not when thousands of people wake up at once, demanding answers. I mean... Isn't that all Margaret ever wanted?*

They stand and watch the men argue. Ava still clings to Markus, nodding at everything he says. Kaarina reaches into her pocket and fishes out two white pills. She stares at them resting on her open palm. Luna investigates her face, trying to figure out what she's thinking. Something tells her the moment's private, too important for her to tap and ask.

Kaarina throws the pills into her mouth, swallows them down. She nods at the CS-key in Luna's hands. "Is that the button?"

Luna hands the computer to her and nods. "The green one. Yes."

They stand and listen to the men shouting at each other, Kaarina's finger hovering above the button. When Yeti leans against a stasis capsule and starts banging his head against it, Kaarina shoves the CS-key at Luna.

"You do it. I can't."

Luna takes the computer. Before she can stop and think about it, she presses the green button.

Markus's whole body freezes. Then he grasps at his head, screaming in agony. His body folds in half, and he kneels on the floor. Then all goes quiet. Ava stares in horror. They all do.

Then Markus lifts his gaze—his eyes glowing with a strange blue light.

"Markus?" Kaarina's voice is just a whisper. "Markus what's going on?"

With robotic, inhuman steps, he walks to the sandwich tray and picks up the kitchen knife. Luna tries to scream, but it's like her whole body is paralyzed. She hugs the CS-key against her stomach and stares, uncomprehending.

"Ava, move!" Yeti has time to turn around but

doesn't reach them quickly enough. Markus lifts the kitchen knife, stabs Ava in the throat. Blood erupts as Ava clutches her throat, trying to stop the bleeding, then falls to her knees gurgling. Her head hits the floor as the life slowly fades from her shocked eyes.

Luna's scream fills the room. Kaarina gasps next to her, while Bill and Micky dart away from Markus and bolt across the room, slipping on the bloody floor.

Yeti charges at Markus, catching him by surprise. The kitchen knife falls to the floor, and Markus falls too. Yeti pins the possessed man against the yellow tiles. He fumbles for the knife and lifts it up in the air.

"No!" Kaarina runs over and grabs Yeti's hand.

"Let go, Kaarina! He's not Markus anymore!" Yeti yells.

"No, you can't kill him!"

When the knife falls to the floor, Yeti lifts Markus up, pinning his hands behind his back. Markus doesn't scramble or try to get away. His dead neon-blue eyes just stare off into space. Yeti shoves him in the closest stasis capsule and locks the door. "Quick! Luna! Bring me some rope!"

Luna turns and runs to the storage space that has been her office for the last few days. She pulls open drawers, letting them drop to the floor and pour out their contents onto the yellow tiles. Finally, she finds the bundles of rope, packed away in one of the storage chests. She picks out as many bundles as she can, grabs a toolbox, and runs back to Yeti.

Yeti wraps a rope around the capsule where Markus's static body stands.

"What the hell happened?" Yeti asks Luna. "Is the city shut down?"

"I don't know! I don't know."

"Well have a fucking guess, would you?"

"They... maybe... Could it be a failsafe? In case someone tries to switch off the city?"

"You're seriously asking me? Come on!"

"They... they must have figured it out. Used the switch against us." She taps the CS-key in her hands. "The code didn't trigger City of Finland, but something else."

"Not something else," Kaarina says, tears streaming down her face. "But *someone*. Look."

Luna looks in the direction where Kaarina's finger points: Mrs. Salonen and the three other Chipped leaders in the capsules. All their eyes shine with neon colors.

"This is what Margaret meant," Kaarina says."The memory stick. She said, 'Use it when those who you trust the most turn against you.' Maybe the stick overrides whatever's taken them over? We must try it. We must wake up Mrs. Salonen. She's the only one who can fix this."

Then the sound reaches their ears. Screams. From upstairs, where the kids are having breakfast burritos with their guardians. Chipped and Unchipped alike.

Yeti takes two long strides toward the basement staircase. "Fuck! It's happening upstairs too!" He waves at them, gesturing for them to hurry. "The kids, we need to help them! All the Chipped must be controlled by Doctor Solomon."

Bill and Micky come back from their hiding place. Micky joins Yeti, but Bill steps to Luna's side. "I'll stay with her. In case... Like mother like daughter."

"Don't let her out of the capsule until her eyes are a normal color," Kaarina says. Then they all race toward the staircase. Running footsteps thump against the basement ceiling. At least the children are now running away to hide from their possessed guardians.

When it's just the two of them, Bill digs out his CS-key. He's hidden it under his sweater. Luna looks at the screen; it's a list of hundreds of items. Food, medicine, construction supply. It's the order Bill said he sent out to the black market days ago.

He presses the send button and sets the computer on the floor. Then he reaches for the toolbox by the rope bundles and takes out a hammer. Bill smashes the CS-key into a shapeless lump.

"What's that all about?" Luna asks.

Bill looks at her, slightly out of breath. "The supply order. I said I sent it in, but I never did."

Luna stares at him, speechless again.

"That's right. How shitty is that? And that's not all. I've used it to call the home base in California. Thought about going back, actually."

Luna frowns. Her hand wraps around the AR-glasses in her pocket.

Bill raises his palms. "I know, I know. But you can judge me later. Let's wake this granny up first."

Luna hands the AR-glasses to Bill, the ones Jovan gave her to stay in touch. Her ticket home to City of Serbia. "While you're at it... could you get rid of these too?"

He stares at the device for a moment. Then, without a word, Bill smashes the AR-glasses into small pieces. Then he grabs a rope and wraps it around Mrs. Salonen's capsule. Luna follows his example, and soon all four stasis capsules are secured with something other than Chipped technology.

Bill turns around. "Do it now. But wait to see if her eyes change color."

"And if they don't?"

"Then we're screwed."

Luna looks over to Markus, staring at her friend in his prison. No, not her friend—something else. A machine. Controlled by some secret command given by the Chip System only a brief moment ago. Solomon has turned Markus into a mindless killer. Why would Mrs. Salonen turn out any different?

Luna keeps staring at Mrs. Salonen. What if she's just as cruel as her daughter? If they bring the old woman back, will she agree to help them? This founder was the mastermind behind the Happiness-Program, even more so than Solomon. But if she agrees with everything Solomon is doing, why would her daughter have locked her away like this?

Luna enters the memory stick into the capsule base. She steps back and stands next to Bill. Without thinking about it, she grabs Bill's hand and squeezes it. He squeezes back.

At first, nothing happens. Then, the blue glow in Mrs. Salonen's eyes slowly fades. Soon, her eyes are soft and friendly, moving ever so faintly. She blinks but then closes her eyes like she's falling asleep again.

"Is the stick doing that?" Bill asks.

"Must be... I have no idea what the hell that code does."

"*Luna, Bill,*" Kaarina's voice echoes in their heads. "*The Chipped have all gone crazy. We've gathered most of the kids, but I can't get to Sanna and Owena. It's Niina, she... she's locked up in their cabin. Eyes glowing, but she's not hurting them. It's like she's possessed, but protecting the girls, instead of killing them. We're in the kitchen, secure for now, but you must hurry. Yeti can't hold them—*"

The purple CS-key in her hand blazes to life, vibrating and buzzing madly. Startled, Luna drops it on the floor and loses the connection with Kaarina. The computer lands screen up, but doesn't break. A purple light appears above it. The hologram starts to form, pixel by pixel, showing off first the sensible lab shoes, then the matching white lab coat. Soon, a smiling woman with a white doctor's coat stands in front of them. The color of her eyes matches Mrs. Salonen's; her white ponytail resembles the old woman's hair. She stares right at Luna. Can she see her?

"So," Doctor Solomon says. "Here we are."

"You sick fuck," Bill hisses at the hologram. "Is this your vision of a better world? Turning people into mindless murderers?"

The doctor's smile deepens. Her eyes blinking softly, she shakes her head. "Oh, William. Always so black and white. Let's face it; you did this to yourselves. I never told you to come after me. If you hadn't hacked into our system, poked around in files that were none of your business... well, do you think any of this would have happened?"

Bill swallows loudly and looks at Ava's body on the floor, only a few feet away. Just like Luna, he can't seem to bear to look at their dead friend. "No. You did this. You're the murderer. You are killing innocent children as we speak. How does that fit into your Happiness-Program?"

"It doesn't, that's how. You know the program is for those who live in the cities, William dear. And you left. Dennis Jenkins had a spot in the sun for you. A glorious apartment with a view. A self-driving limo, a dream job, everything you ever wanted out of life. And you threw it all away, and for what? To join a silly rebel girl who thought it would be fun to play war?"

"Fun?" Luna leans in and stares into the hologram's eyes. "You think this is *fun* for us? People are dying!"

"Tell me this, sweetheart. Were people dying yesterday?"

Luna and Bill both stay quiet, reluctant to answer

any question Solomon throws at them.

"Exactly," she says. "No one was dying until you stuck your nose into files and programs that were absolutely none of your business."

"Is that what Mrs. Salonen did?" Luna asks, desperate to think anything but the fact that the doctor might be right. That they themselves are to blame. "Is that why you locked her away and left her to rot? Your own mother?"

For a moment, Luna sees a trace of surprise on Laura Solomon's face. "So that's where you are, then. Iceland." Her calm and soft expression returns. She starts tapping and swiping her invisible keyboard, a satisfied smile deepening on her face. "How is the resort these days? It's been years since I've visited."

"It's better for some of us. Those who are not locked up in a hell-tube," Bill says. "What did Mama Bear do to you anyway? I always figured crazy-ass dictators like you would have daddy issues, but clearly, you're more fucked up than we thought. Killing someone who gave you life."

"Killing?" Solomon leans over to a screen behind her, taps on what seems like a different keyboard than the one she's been working with. After a pause, she says, "No, says right here. Her stasis capsule hasn't been opened since 2085. My mother's exactly where she's supposed to be. And she's very much alive."

"She's as good as dead and you know it," Luna says. "You evil fuck-face."

"Well, there you go again. Sticking your nose in our family business. A matter that has nothing to do with any of you. Don't worry about my dear old mother. I can assure you she'll stay under my control. Just like your other Chipped friends. Speaking of which, how is Mister Nyman doing these days?"

Bill and Luna can't help but look at Markus, stored inside a stasis capsule with a rope around it. The tinted glass shows his silhouette and a pair of glowing neon-blue eyes.

"He always had the kindest eyes, that boy. Gorgeously striking blue, especially at the moment, don't you think? See, at first I didn't like it. When I noticed how the gene expression that followed this particular chip update caused their eyes to glow. And then... well it started to grow on me."

"Luna, look!" Bill says silently, tapping Luna so Doctor Solomon can't hear. Luna looks in the direction Bill's pointing; at Mrs. Salonen. The old woman's eyes are open again. They don't emit an unnatural light. Her eyes move from side to side, slowly, as if she's trying to figure out where she is. What year it is. Why she's locked in a machine she once created. Luna feels bad for her, and at the same time, she wishes the woman would snap out of it faster. Be more efficient. Help them destroy her own flesh and blood.

"Well, my loves," Doctor Solomon's hologram says. "It's been a pleasure chatting with you. But I need to let you go now. Much to do, you see."

"And who are your Chipped minions killing in the city?" Bill asks. "If you need suggestions, I'd recommend a certain nurse who can't keep her mouth shut."

Solomon laughs, reaching for something they can't see in the hologram. Soon the AR-glasses appear on her face. "Nurse Saarinen is only doing her job. If I'm not wrong, it was your precious Kaarina who spilled the beans. You got pretty close, I'll give you that. Too bad your leader is a half-witted barn worker who shouldn't be in charge of anything more complicated than shoveling manure."

"Don't talk about her like that!" Bill and Luna say in sync. This makes Solomon laugh even more.

"Such innocence. Such inanity. One thing I'll give Kaarina, she's really got you all brainwashed." Solomon shakes her head and sighs. "It's a shame, really. With your skillsets, many of you would have excelled in the city. And yet, here we are. You, floundering in what you call war and what I call an after-thought."

"If we're such a nullity, why slaughter us?" Bill says. "Whatever you did to the Chipped, make them stop. People don't have to die."

Solomon shrugs at Bill's words. "As I said, dear. You brought this on. Not me. Now, excuse me. I'm running late for a board meeting."

"Wait."

Bill looks at Luna, tapping her, but she blocks the connection. There's no time. They need Solomon to turn off the nanobots. If she doesn't, they're all as good as dead.

"What if I were to tell you your mother is awake?"

Solomon's head tilts, but she doesn't take off the AR-glasses. "That's cute, my dear. But it's a bit too late for bluffing, don't you think?" She turns to shut down the connection.

"Margaret Wilson," Luna says quickly. At her words, Solomon freezes again. She turns and takes off her glasses. "Okay," she says, forcing a small smile. "You have my attention."

Luna swallows and dodges Bill's gaze. He wouldn't approve of her plan, if he knew what she was about to do. If what she's thinking can be called a plan. She's winging it. But if they lose Solomon now, they'll lose Markus and possibly everyone else in Iceland for good. Yeti is strong and knows how to fight, but there's only one of him, against dozens of murderous Chipped.

"She gave me a code. Margaret. A code and a memory stick."

All trace of amusement and calm disappears from Solomon's face. Her eyes turn cold, her lips press into a thin line. "Did she, now?"

"Yeah, she did. And I know it can open her stasis capsule and free her from whatever sickness you've laid upon the Chipped. I know because we've already done it. We've already woken up Mrs. Salonen."

Doctor Solomon's face relaxes. She doesn't smile but rolls her eyes quickly. "See, now I know you're bluffing.

Didn't I just tell you I checked her capsule door? It hasn't been opened for years."

"That's only because we tied a rope around it," Bill says and steps closer to Mrs. Salonen. The old woman's blurred eyes lock on Bill. When he raises his hand and waves it in front of her eyes, Mrs. Salonen blinks twice.

"A rope? What good would that do?"

"We weren't sure if pulling the switch would open them," Luna says and then shakes her head. "Doesn't matter. She's here now. Wide awake."

Solomon stands up, the hologram now only showing the back of her white doctor's coat. Wordlessly, she puts on the AR-glasses, tapping and swiping the air again.

"You can't reverse this," Bill says. "We know how to take off the chipping helmet too. We've done that before."

Solomon doesn't reply.

Luna walks over to Bill and reaches for the rope. *Are we sure she'll be on our side?*

"She fucking better be. And if she's not... how much worse can this get?"

Luna nods at Bill. They loosen the rope. Solomon taps and swipes, her fingers working unnaturally fast on her invisible keyboard.

The rope falls to the floor. When Luna looks up, Mrs. Salonen stares straight at her. Her lip twitches half an inch, her eyes blink slowly. She's coming to her senses.

"You really thought you could beat me, didn't you?"

Luna turns around and sees Solomon sitting again. Her face is calm and expressionless once more.

"We'll beat your ass any day," Bill says, smiling. "You sick fuck."

Solomon smiles, then turns to reach for a screen next to her. She taps on a button, then turns to face them again. "Then tell me this, sweethearts."

The speakers at the ceiling crackle to life. Outside, the sirens do the same.

A sharp pain travels across Luna's body, from the back of her head all the way to her toes. A high-pitch sound rings in her ears, filling her head with agony. Bill grunts and holds his head next to her. He can feel it too. Agony, surging through his brain. His veins. His whole being.

"Did you think that just because I can't fully access your brain implant… I wouldn't be able to have a little fun with it?" Doctor Solomon's voice booms in the room.

The room spins. Luna supports herself against Mrs. Salonen's capsule. The old woman observes her through the glass, confusion in her eyes.

"Not that you'd think to consider something like this. I mean, that's something a smart person would do. To think about what it means. To have a piece of technology inside your head… technology that I created."

Bill falls on the floor. He crawls on all fours until he collapses, motionless, against the yellow tiles.

Luna's knees give out. When she crumples to the floor, she hears dull thumps upstairs, as the Unchipped people, hiding in the kitchen above, crash down unconscious.

Doctor Solomon's laughter seems to come from under water. Her words slur in Luna's ears. She gives in and lies down on the floor, still watching Mrs. Salonen's face. The woman's hand twitches, and her head moves an inch under the helmet.

"See my dears? This so-called war was never yours to win. Because how can you win a war in a reality where you don't even exist? Sure, I can't access the failing chips in your heads, but it doesn't mean that I don't know a thing or two about the Unchipped brain. It's amazing what you can do with a lab full of test subjects such as yourself. That high pitch sound you hear? Might not be the loveliest sensation, I'm sure, but don't you worry... this audio frequency is known to turn the Unchipped mind right off. And it's going to happen right about... now."

Just before she closes her eyes, Luna sees the capsule door open. A bare foot steps down. A yellow tile lights up.

CHAPTER 5
MRS. SALONEN

The tile floor feels cold under my bare feet. I stand, supporting my drenched frame on my own invention as I pull the various tubes, needles, and catheters from my body. Piece after piece, it all comes back to me.

Suicides.

Mass shootings.

People spitting in each other's faces.

Vans driven into crowds of protesters.

A healing helmet. A healing capsule. A healing program. A hope for *happiness*.

Legs wobbling under my body weight, I let go of the capsule. Carefully, one inch at a time, I turn and stare at what has been my prison for… how many years have I lost? One? Ten? Fifty?

The chipping helmet rests lopsided inside the pod. A faint layer of condensation covers the glass walls beside it. From my breath. I never died, though my head and body feel too light and thin to be alive. I take a step closer. My hand shaking, I reach for the glass door. It closes with a faint click.

In the dim yellow light, I look around the room. The air is cold against my naked body. A hint of embarrassment crosses my mind, but I reject that worry. Feeling embarrassed is a luxury I can't afford at this moment. There are more pressing things to consider now. I know this, but my mind refuses to let it all flow back into my consciousness. It's too much to take in.

I blink and see lifeless bodies lying on the floor. The man's face is covered with long, blood-stained dreadlocks. The girl, delicate but clearly strong, rests next to him, collapsed in a pool of blood and a device I faintly recognize. A few feet away, another girl. This one even younger.

"Hmm." My throat refuses anything more. Everything aches. Even my fingernails, my hair. My body screams for water.

I take a step to turn around. A few feet away from my prison, a young man with unnaturally blue eyes stares at me, locked inside a capsule identical to mine. An android? The rest of him doesn't look like a robot, just his neon eyes. He's not wearing a chipping helmet, though. And the pod is wrapped with multiple layers of rope.

"Mm."

Left foot, right foot. The wobble gets worse. Pause and wait. I regard him, a beautiful man with wild hair. Why does he have clothes on? Is he a prisoner here, like me?

I turn slowly, taking in the room. Empty capsules are all around. Then, next to mine, three more pods with ropes around them. A low humming fills the air, finally reaching my ears and entering my mind. Reality seems blurry. So fragile. If I snapped my fingers it would all shatter and crash down in front of me. Like a thin glass with too much weight on top.

The silhouettes inside the capsules are too blurred for me to recognize. But the long black hair is familiar. So is the bushy beard, and finally the strong jawline.

"Ah."

The founders. Not all of us, but a few. What brings us together today? Here. Underground and banished. Turned off like yesterday's technology or a medical research site without government funding. Turnips. Rotten potatoes.

What brings us together?

Right foot. Left foot. Right. Pause. I'm almost at the girl's side, the one with a face so sharp you can't miss her intelligence. A young mind. Hope. Love. Everything that humanity needs, if it hopes to recover from…

My mind blocks the thought before I can hold onto it.

What is this? Why am I here? Naked. Wilted. Muddled.

As I lower my body down, I prepare to feel a sharp pain travel from my left hip to my right.

But the pain never arrives.

Physical discomfort is suddenly just a memory from yesterday. Or last year? I close my mind and hang onto the memory. First, all I hear is a low hum. Then my ears start ringing. Breathing steadily, calming my shaking body, I push deeper into the past.

A thunder of galloping hooves.

A doodle. A chicken without an egg.

A meeting room with a round table.

And a woman, with a blonde ponytail. No, not a woman. Just a girl. My *Laura*.

My eyes fly open, and I stare at the CS-key under the fallen girl. Slowly moving closer to her in the yellow light, I reach to try her pulse. Slow. But she's alive.

I pull the computer from underneath her. The screen flickers with purple light, numbers and letters flashing by. I push a button in the middle. A purple light appears, streaming out of the CS-key. I hold it, my hands shaking and my breath shallow.

Lab shoes.

A white coat.

Sharp eyes—the same shade as mine.

I stare at the hologram that is my daughter. She tilts her head, listening. Waiting.

The words get stuck in my throat. Swallowing hurts but clears my throat enough for me to wheeze the words out.

"What have you done?"

Her chin lifts several inches. The sharpness of her eyes becomes clearer. Laura's serious face stares right at me, without seeing a thing. But she doesn't have to see me. She'd recognize my voice even with her eyes shut. The voice that once sang her lullabies and spoke comforting words.

But when she talks, I hardly recognize her. Her voice is too cold. Lost. Too machine-like to be my baby girl.

"Hello, mother."

Shoot! Book 5 of the Unchipped story is at a close. But don't worry, you can find out what happens next in Book 6 in the Unchipped series, ~~UNCHIPPED:~~ LAURA available on Amazon

My dearest reader,

You are simply amazing! Thank you so much for your support and readership! I can't tell you how much you reading this book means to me. I'm humbled and honored that you've dedicated your valuable time to experience the Unchipped universe with me. I'm still a newbie author, so if you were to leave me a review on Amazon it would be a huge help! Short or long, doesn't matter. Reviews are the best way to help other readers find the Unchipped Series.

Want to stay in touch? I would love it if you'd subscribe to my newsletter @ www.TayaDeVere.com/HappinessProgram

Starting in August 2020, newsletter subscribers will receive free, exclusive early access to in-universe short stories from the Unchipped series a week before each book comes out. That's every eighteen days so be sure to sign up to get first crack at the series!

Facebook – facebook.com/tayadevereauthor
Instagram – instagram.com/tayadevere_author
Goodreads – goodreads.com/tayadevere
Bookbub – bookbub.com/authors/taya-devere
Amazon – amazon.com/Taya-DeVere/e/B07KRJPMTV

Gratefully yours,
Taya DeVere

THE END

About the Author

Taya is a Finnish-American author, writing contemporary fiction and dystopian sci-fi. After living and traveling in America for seven years, she now lives in Finland with her husband Chris, their dog Seamus, three bunny-boys (Ronin, Baby, Loki), and her horse of a lifetime, Arabella.

Best things in life: friends & family, memories made, and mistakes to learn from. Taya also loves licorice ice cream, secondhand clothes and things, bunny sneezes, salmiakki, and sauna.

Dislikes: clowns, the Muppets, Moomin trolls, dolls (especially porcelain dolls), human size mascots and celery.

Taya's writing is inspired by the works of authors like Margaret Atwood, Peter Heller, Hugh Howey, and C.M. Martens.

Final Thanks

When I tell someone I write books for a living, people tend to ask me two questions.

1. How do you come up with story ideas?

2. Are your characters based on real people?

I guess the answer to both questions is the same.

All my stories are more or less inspired by people I've met in real life. I've always been fascinated by different kinds of personalities, even before I left Finland and moved to the United Kingdom and later on to America. Especially people who are somewhat odd and don't seem to fit in tickle my imagination.

And therefore, I would like to thank my friends, who are the true fuel behind my storytelling. Plots, scenes, characters... At the end of the day, it's all based on real life—real people. Even those whom I've lost touch with, or only enjoy a cup of coffee once a year (or ten years), I value my tribe more than anything else.

So, thank you; Sonja, Suvi, Heikki, Johanna, Minja, Niina, Outi, Piritta, Luna, Sari, Jackie, Kate, Andrea, Jason, Pippa, Shannon, Eero, and Sybille. You make my world (the real one, and the ones I create) go round.

The Unchipped series – Release schedule 2020
UNCHIPPED: KAARINA - 8/31/2020
UNCHIPPED: WILLIAM - 9/18/2020
UNCHIPPED: ENYD - 10/6/2020
UNCHIPPED: LUNA - 10/24/2020
UNCHIPPED: THE RESORT - 11/11/2020
~~UN~~CHIPPED: LAURA - 11/30/2020
~~UN~~CHIPPED: DENNIS - 12/18/2020